APACHE VENDETTA

The brothers were huffing and cursing. They must have figured it would be easy with two against one.

Fargo was happy to disappoint them. A fist clipped his cheek and he smashed his forearm into Gant's mouth. Link swung at his neck but missed. Fargo kicked Link in the knee and, when Link doubled over, kneed him in the face.

"Stop it, all of you!" Tandy yelled.

Fargo was vaguely aware of other voices and a commotion but he didn't take his eyes off the Bascombs. To keep them from setting themselves he unleashed a flurry, hitting first one and then the other, going for the face and the gut. Their jaws were iron; they wouldn't go down that way.

THE TRAILSMAN
#387

APACHE
VENDETTA
by
Jon Sharpe

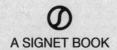

A SIGNET BOOK

SIGNET
Published by the Penguin Group
Penguin Group (USA) LLC, 375 Hudson Street,
New York, New York 10014

USA | Canada | UK | Ireland | Australia | New Zealand | India | South Africa | China
penguin.com
A Penguin Random House Company

First published by Signet, an imprint of New American Library,
a division of Penguin Group (USA) LLC

First Printing, January 2014

The first chapter of this book previously appeared in *Nevada Vipers' Nest*, the three
hundred eighty-sixth volume in this series.

 REGISTERED TRADEMARK—MARCA REGISTRADA

ISBN 978-0-451-46601-3

Printed in the United States of America
10 9 8 7 6 5 4 3 2 1

The Trailsman

Beginnings . . . they bend the tree and they mark the man. Skye Fargo was born when he was eighteen. Terror was his midwife, vengeance his first cry. Killing spawned Skye Fargo, ruthless, cold-blooded murder. Out of the acrid smoke of gunpowder still hanging in the air, he rose, cried out a promise never forgotten.

The Trailsman they began to call him all across the West: searcher, scout, hunter, the man who could see where others only looked, his skills for hire but not his soul, the man who lived each day to the fullest, yet trailed each tomorrow. Skye Fargo, the Trailsman, the seeker who could take the wildness of a land and the wanting of a woman and make them his own.

1861, New Mexico Territory—no one stops an Apache out for vengeance.

1

Skye Fargo was being shadowed. To have that happen in Blackfoot or Sioux country would be bad. But now he was in Apache territory, and that was worse. No other tribe could hold a candle to the Apaches when it came to a silent stalk and kill.

Fargo wasn't there by choice. Colonel Hastings at Fort Union had sent for him, saying it was urgent he get there as quickly as possible.

So here Fargo was, pushing his Ovaro hard over the rugged Southwest terrain in the height of summer. The heat was blistering.

Fargo was a big man, with eyes as blue as a high country lake and as piercing as a hawk's. Broad of shoulder and packed with muscle, he wore buckskins and a red bandanna and a Colt high on his hip.

Fort Union was situated on the Santa Fe Trail, on the west side of a valley watered by a creek. It was built to protect travelers from hostiles, particularly the Jicarilla Apaches, who keenly resented the white invasion of their land and took great delight in ending the life of any white they caught.

And now at least three of them were stalking him.

Fargo had caught on to them by a fluke when he'd stopped to rest at a spring and climbed some boulders to scout the lay of the land ahead. For the briefest instant he'd glimpsed a trio of swarthy forms and then they had melted away. It was a rare mistake on their part.

They were on foot but that hardly mattered. Apaches could run all day and be fresh to run again the next morning. He might outdistance them by riding the stallion into the ground but then they would catch up and he'd be no better off.

So Fargo was being careful not to let the heat take too much of a toll. His eyes under his hat brim were always in motion, flicking right and left and up and ahead, and he often gave quick glances back.

The Apaches hadn't made the same mistake twice. They rarely did. But they were still there, still stalking him. He knew it as surely as he'd ever known anything.

Fargo had tangled with Apaches before. They were some of the most formidable warriors alive, and devious as hell. Masters in the art of dispensing death, they had tricks up their sleeves that no one had ever heard of.

Extra cause for Fargo to be extra alert. It was a strain, and kept his nerves on edge. Any sound, however slight, caused him to stiffen.

By his reckoning he was a day out of the fort. The sun was about to set, and although he'd like to push on, the Ovaro was lathered with sweat and needed rest. So against his better judgment he sought a spot to stop for the night.

The mountains were as dry as a desert and as wild as the warriors they bred, a hard land with a lot of rock and sparse vegetation.

Fargo had been through this area before and knew of a tank midway along a ridge. Massive boulders hid it. Once among them, he was in welcome shade. The smell of the water brought the Ovaro's head up and made him lick his dry lips in anticipation. But he didn't dare relax. The Apaches were bound to know of the tank, too.

Under the sprawl of giant monoliths, the pool gleamed dusky in the twilight.

Fargo dismounted and stretched and let the stallion dip its muzzle. His hand on his Colt, he studied the soft earth at the tank's edge. Deer had been there, and a bobcat. There wasn't a single moccasin print but that didn't mean a thing. Apaches never left tracks if they could help it.

Fargo debated whether to strip his saddle and decided not to. He might need to light a shuck in a hurry. Sliding his Henry rifle from the scabbard, he worked the lever to feed a cartridge into the chamber and sat cross-legged with his back to a boulder where he could watch the open space below the tank and the land beyond.

Its thirst quenched, the Ovaro wearily hung its head and dozed.

The last gray of twilight faded and darkness spread. Coyotes greeted the night with keening wails. An owl hooted, and once, in the distance, a mountain lion screamed.

All normal sounds of a normal night.

Fargo didn't let it lull his guard. The Apaches were out there, waiting for their chance.

He fought to stay awake. Over the past three days he'd barely had three hours of sleep each night and it was taking a toll. Again and again his eyelids grew leaden and his chin dipped to his chest. Again and again he jerked his head up and shook himself.

In the middle of the night a meteor streaked the sky. Some would take that as a bad omen but he wasn't the superstitious sort. He didn't believe black cats were evil, either. Or that breaking a mirror brought seven years' bad luck.

His one exception was Lady Luck at the poker table. If he had a mistress, it would be her. What he wouldn't give to be playing cards in a saloon somewhere, and sipping fine whiskey. Maybe with a friendly dove at his side. He hadn't been in a saloon in weeks and missed it dearly.

About two hours before sunrise his chin dipped once more, and this time he succumbed to the deep sleep of exhaustion.

A whinny brought Fargo awake with a start. His befuddled brain took note of a pink gleam to the east and the chill morning air, and then he snapped fully awake as he realized he wasn't alone.

The three Apaches had taken advantage of his lapse. They weren't ten feet away and one had a rifle pointed at his chest.

2

Fargo was as good as dead. He could try to raise the Henry but the Apache would put a slug into him the instant he moved. The other two had rifles, as well, but theirs were in the crook of their arms.

All three were what whites would call typical: swarthy and stocky with broad faces, wearing breechclouts and knee-high moccasins. All had headbands, and knives.

Fargo wondered why he was still alive. They could easily have killed him while he slept. Then again, Apaches were notorious for doing things to captives that gave peaceable folks nightmares.

The warrior holding the rifle showed no inclination to shoot. He just stood there and stared, and then he said in English, "Put long gun down."

After a moment's hesitation, Fargo did. He still had his Colt and could draw it quicker than they could blink.

The warrior with the rifle nodded at the other two and they advanced.

Fargo tensed, thinking they were about to seize him. But no. They walked past him, squatted at the tank, and dipped their hands in the water. His surprise must have shown.

"We only want drink," the Apache pointing the rifle informed him.

"Well, now," Fargo said. This was as close to a miracle as he'd ever come.

"I Culebra Negro," the warrior said.

Fargo grunted. Apaches never gave their real names. They thought it gave others power over them, so they used Spanish names instead. This one was Black Snake.

"You be He Who Walks Many Trails."

Fargo was startled. "How do you know that?" It was a name some tribes knew him by, but not, to his knowledge, the Apaches.

Culebra Negro smiled. "Know many things. Know you be at fort before day done."

Fargo glanced at the other two, who were regarding him with what he took to be curiosity.

"You have good horse," Culebra Negro said. "Good guns."

Here it came, Fargo thought. They had been playing with him and now they would bare their fangs. But no. The other two moved back and one trained a rifle on him while Culebra Negro lowered his and stepped to the tank. He seemed greatly amused.

"Have I met you somewhere?" Fargo asked, knowing full well he never had.

"No."

"Then why are you being so nice?"

Culebra Negro snorted, the Apache equivalent of a cackle. "I never nice to whites."

"I'm still breathing," Fargo pointed out. It was a stupid thing to say. It might provoke them. But damn, none of this made sense.

"You not like breathing?"

Now Fargo was sure that Culebra Negro was inwardly laughing at him. "I like it as much as I liked the Apache gal I stayed with once."

About to dip his hand in, Culebra Negro paused, his dark eyes glittering. "You had Shis-Inday woman?"

As Fargo was aware, "Shis-Inday" was the Apache name for themselves. It meant "men of the woods." "She and me had each other a lot."

Culebra Negro's lips quirked in a cold smile. "I like to cut your throat."

Now Fargo had done it. He started to inch his fingers closer to his Colt.

"But him say not to, so we don't."

"Him?" Fargo said.

Culebra Negro wet his lips and took a single swallow from

5

his cupped hand, and stood. Wheeling, he strode past Fargo and on down the slope, the other two backing after him. At the bottom Culebra Negro stopped and looked up.

"We see you get to fort."

"You what?" Fargo asked in confusion.

"We keep you safe from other Shis-Inday."

Fargo was dumbfounded. They were *escorting* him. He'd never heard of such a thing. "What did I do to deserve this?"

"You find out soon enough," Culebra Negro said, and he gave another snort and walked on.

Fargo sat there as the sky slowly brightened and a golden arch crowned the new day. He'd had his share of strange things happen but this just about beat them all. Apaches being sociable was as unlikely as being invited to tea by a grizzly.

Yet he was still alive.

"I'll be damned," he said.

3

Fort Union was pretty much as Fargo remembered.

There was no palisade and the buildings were made of logs, not adobe as at some forts. Rumor had it the army was unhappy with the site and planned to relocate. They did that a lot. Built posts where it was too damp or there was too little water or it was too difficult to defend, and then had to build another in a better spot.

Fort Union was all three.

Sentries were posted, and the one who challenged Fargo did so in a bored I-can-see-you're-a-white-man sort of way and waved him on.

Soldiers were drilling on the parade ground. Others were digging a trench, probably for a latrine, while yet more were up on a roof doing God knew what.

Fargo wearily drew rein at a hitch rail in front of the company headquarters and dismounted. He'd made good time and it was several hours yet to sundown. Twice he'd glimpsed his escorts, the last time half a mile from the fort.

A young orderly jumped up when he told who he was. "The colonel has been waiting for you to arrive. I'll announce you."

"Don't bother," Fargo said. "I'm acquainted with the gent." Before the young soldier could object, he strode into the commander's office without knocking.

Colonel James Hastings was at his desk, scribbling a report. Gray at the temples, his uniform clean and pressed, even seated he bore himself in military fashion, sitting ramrod straight. He beamed and came out of his chair as if propelled from a catapult. "Skye! Thank God you finally got here."

"Finally, hell," Fargo said as he shook hands. "I'm about tuckered out."

Colonel Hastings motioned at a chair. "Have a seat, then, and we'll get right to it."

"To what, exactly?" Fargo said as he sank down. "All I was told was that you needed to see me in a hurry."

Instead of sitting back down, Hastings clasped his hands behind his back as if he were at parade rest. "I have a tinder-box on my hands and I'm hoping you can snuff the tinder."

"Before you go on, I can use a drink."

Colonel Hastings opened a drawer and produced a silver flask. "I shouldn't, but you're entitled." He passed it across. "Now, then—"

Fargo held up a hand. He uncapped the flask, tilted it to his mouth, and took a long, slow swallow. When he lowered it he smiled and let out an "Ahhhh."

"Happy now?"

"I'm obliged."

Hastings chuckled. "As I was about to say, I take it you've heard of Cuchillo Colorado?"

Fargo nodded. The name meant Red Knife. For several years now, Cuchillo Colorado and his band had been the scourge of the territory. "They say he likes to hang people upside down over a fire and boil their brains."

Colonel Hastings frowned. "I'm afraid that's true. He's conducted a relentless campaign against white homesteads and settlements. Before we came along, he did the same with the Mexicans."

"He hates everybody who isn't Apache," Fargo said. There were a lot like that.

"I understand you met him once."

"I'd recollect if I had." Fargo took another swig of Monongahela and reluctantly capped the flask and set it on the desk.

"Perhaps I misunderstood," Colonel Hastings said. Turning to a rack, he retrieved his hat. "Come with me, if you will, and we'll clarify things."

The orderly stood when the colonel emerged and Hastings said, "At ease, Private."

After his brief spell indoors, the heat hit Fargo like a furnace. "I need to stable my horse," he mentioned as Hastings led him along the parade ground.

"First things first," Hastings said. "It won't take long. I promise."

Fargo shrugged. Once he bedded the Ovaro down, he planned to rustle up a bottle and relax for a while. He owed it to himself after the ordeal of getting there.

"For all his viciousness, Cuchillo Colorado is widely respected by his people and those of other bands," Colonel Hastings was saying as he strode toward a small building next to the sutler's.

"He's respected *because* of it," Fargo corrected him.

"As may be," Colonel Hastings said. "You can imagine how the army has made stopping his depredations a top priority."

Fargo thought he knew where their talk was going. "In other words, they want him dead."

"We did," Hastings said. He came to a door, knocked once, and opened it. "After you," he said.

Fargo stepped inside and barely had time to register a small room with a figure in a shadowed corner when the figure sprang at him and the tip of a knife was pressed to his throat.

4

Fargo reacted on pure instinct. Even as the figure sprang, his hand swooped to his Colt. In a blur he had it out and cocked.

"No!" Colonel Hastings cried.

Fargo's attacker froze. A craggy face, the barrel chest, the breechclout and the moccasins, to say nothing of the long knife with its red hilt, were enough for Fargo to guess, "You'd be Cuchillo Colorado, I take it?"

The Apache leader glanced down at the Colt pressed to his ribs and did a strange thing—he smiled. "We meet once more, Skye Fargo," he said in much better English than Culebra Negro used. Stepping back, he sheathed his blade and folded his arms across his chest.

"Damn, that was close," Colonel Hastings declared. "Why'd you jump at him like that? I knocked, didn't I?"

"I did not know who knocked and I am among enemies," Cuchillo Colorado replied without taking his eyes off Fargo.

"I gave you my word no harm would come to you," Colonel Hastings said.

Fargo was puzzled by why the warrior was giving him an intent scrutiny. "What was that about meeting again?"

"You don't remember?" Cuchillo Colorado said, sounding surprised.

"Refresh my memory." Fargo was still holding his Colt and twirled it into his holster with a flourish.

"Two summers ago," Cuchillo Colorado said. "Warm Springs Canyon."

Blood-drenched memories washed over Fargo. Of him helping a patrol track a war party. Of the captain insisting they make camp for the night at Warm Springs in a box canyon, over his objections. Of being attacked at dawn by a band of Apaches, and of being trapped there for three days until he led a breakout. Several troopers lost their lives. "That was your bunch?"

"You did not know?"

"How would I?" Fargo rejoined. During the entire three-day clash he'd caught only glimpses of swarthy ghosts as they flitted from cover to cover.

"You killed two warriors," Cuchillo Colorado reminded him.

"I shot one on a cliff and the other as he was trying to steal our horses," Fargo recollected.

"The blue coats shot but they did not hit us," Cuchillo Colorado said. "You were better."

Fargo returned the compliment with, "It was clever of you, trapping us in the canyon." And damned stupid of the captain to camp there.

"Now we meet again," Cuchillo Colorado said.

"Why?"

"The colonel did not tell you?" Cuchillo Colorado said, sounding surprised.

"I thought he should hear it from you," Hastings said. "So he can judge for himself whether he wants to or not."

"Wants to what?" Fargo asked.

"I would like you to help me," Cuchillo Colorado said.

"Help you *what*, damn it?"

Cuchillo Colorado took a deep breath, as if what he was about to say was painful and he was girding himself.

"Help me find the whites who rape my daughter."

"The curs," Colonel Hastings said.

"She dead now," Cuchillo Colorado said. "She lay in our lodge many days. Bleeding. Hurting. Our medicine man did all he could but she died."

"I'd heard a rumor about it from some Pimas," Colonel Hastings said. "Naturally, I expected Cuchillo Colorado to go on the warpath and kill whites like never before. Instead, out of the blue, he showed up here and asked for my aid in finding the culprits."

"Hold on," Fargo said. "The army has been after him for years. And now you're telling me that you want to work *with* him?"

"Orders from higher up," Hastings said. "I passed on his request and they agreed to his terms."

"Terms?" Fargo repeated.

"In return for our help in tracking down the prospectors who violated his daughter, Cuchillo Colorado has given his word that he won't lift a hand against another white for as long as he lives. The same applies to his entire band."

Fargo couldn't believe what he was hearing.

"I know what you're thinking," Colonel Hastings said. "That we've struck a deal with the devil. But put yourself in our boots. Last year alone his band killed over twenty settlers and others, that we know of. Think of how many lives we can save by putting an end to their hostilities."

"And you're willing to take him at his word?" Fargo asked in amazement.

"I speak with a straight tongue," Cuchillo Colorado interrupted. "If you help me find the men who killed my child, I will wage no more war against your kind forever."

"Hell," Fargo said.

5

Fargo had known the army to do some harebrained things in his time but this took the cake. He was about to tell Hastings that as they left but then he saw that someone was waiting for them.

Hastings didn't notice until he'd shut the door and turned. His face visibly hardened. "Where did you come from, Jaster?" he demanded.

The man called Jaster had a smile that made Fargo think of a weasel. Everything about him was weaselly. From his hair to his overfed body to a face that even a mother wouldn't love. His store-bought suit was rumpled from a lot of wear. His derby had dirt spots. Stubble speckled his chin and he scratched it as he replied, "Is that any way to greet an old friend?"

"I have a lot of friends," Colonel Hastings said, "and you're not one of them."

Jaster laughed. "Could that have anything to do with what I do for a living?" His beady eyes flicked to Fargo. "Why don't you introduce me to the gent beside you?"

"Answer my question," the colonel said.

"My editor sent me to check into rumors he'd heard," Jaster said. "Word is that you've been secretly meeting with Cuchillo Colorado over the past month or more."

Fargo could tell that the officer was taken aback at having word leak out.

Hastings tried to hide his surprise and said, "Your editor heard wrong."

"Did he, indeed?" Jaster said. He jerked his thumb at Fargo. "I'm still waiting for an introduction."

"Skye Fargo," Colonel Hastings said with obvious reluctance, "I'd like you to meet Harold Jaster. He works for *The Guardian*, a Santa Fe newspaper—"

"The most read newspaper in the territory," Jaster boasted.

"—and you can be sure if there is dirt to be dug up about anyone or anything," Hastings went on, "Mr. Jaster, here, will do the digging."

"Damn right I will," Jaster said. "I don't like people keeping secrets."

Fargo had taken an immediate dislike to the man, and said nothing.

Jaster did more chin-scratching. "Fargo, you say? Why is that name familiar?"

"We're busy, Mr. Jaster," Colonel Hastings said. "Come see me at my office in an hour or so and I'll answer any questions you may have."

"I doubt that," Jaster said. "You're never very forthcoming."

"I wonder why," Hastings said.

Jaster focused on Fargo again. "You didn't answer me, mister. Who are you that I think I know your name, and what do you do?"

"Do those ears of yours work?" Fargo asked.

"What?" Jaster reached up and touched one. "Of course they do. Why?"

"Because I'll only say this once." Fargo stepped up to him and Jaster's throat bobbed. "I'm not the colonel. I don't have to be nice to jackasses. Take that as a warning."

"Hey now," Jaster said. "We've only just met and you treat me like I'm a cockroach?"

Fargo strode past without another word. When he reached the hitch rail, he stopped and leaned against it and waited for Hastings, who was arguing heatedly with Jaster. Finally Hastings gestured and Jaster walked off and the colonel crossed to the headquarters building.

"Damn that man, anyhow. He gets my dander up every time."

"Have him thrown off the post," Fargo suggested.

"If only I could. But his editor would complain to the governor, and the next thing I know, I'd have my superiors breathing down my neck." Hastings stared after the journalist, who went into the sutler's. "No, as you said, I have to be polite whether I want to or not. It worries me, though."

"What does?"

"That he'll confirm I've been talking to Cuchillo Colorado and write it. A lot of people would be upset."

"Mad is more like it," Fargo said. Cuchillo Colorado was just about the most despised Apache on the frontier.

"I'm trying to save lives," Colonel Hastings said. "That should count for something."

"Do you really think Cuchillo Colorado will keep his word?"

"Whether I do or I don't is irrelevant," Hastings replied. "My superiors do, and they've ordered me to honor his request." He paused. "And since you're in our employ as a scout, they've ordered you to help him find those who raped his daughter."

"And if I refuse?"

"Then I'm under orders to throw you in the stockade for disobeying a direct order until you come to your senses."

"Well, hell," Fargo said.

6

The collection of structures hardly qualified as a town but it called itself Unionville. It was barely a quarter mile from the fort. In a couple of years it would probably wither away and become yet another ghost town, but at the moment a sign said it had sixty-two souls and at least a third of them were in the saloon.

Fargo paid for a bottle and claimed a corner table for himself. He didn't bother with a glass.

He was in a foul mood. He didn't like this Cuchillo Colorado business. He didn't like it one bit. He liked even less that the army was being so high-handed about it. He had to do as they wanted, or else.

He swirled the whiskey and chugged, and as he set the bottle down, perfume tingled his nose and a shapely vision filled his sight.

"What do we have here? I do declare I've struck the jackpot."

She wasn't much over thirty with blond curls that jiggled when she moved and a dress so tight, it was a wonder it didn't split at the seams. She had green eyes and a fine smile, and tits as big as watermelons.

"I could say the same," Fargo said, and pushed a chair out with his boot. "Join me, why don't you?"

"Gladly," she said, managing it as if she were a queen sitting on a throne. "I'm Tandy, by the way. It's short for Tandoline."

"Do tell," Fargo said. Not that he gave a damn about her name. He was more interested in her tits.

"I don't believe I've seen you in here before."

Fargo slid the bottle across. "Wet your whistle if you'd like."

"Would I?" Tandy said, and damned if she didn't take a long swallow without batting an eye.

"I like a gal who likes to drink."

"I like gents who are easy on the eyes." Tandy looked him up and down. "And, Lordy, you are as easy as they come."

Fargo took the bottle back. "Enough small talk. Where's your room?"

"My goodness," Tandy teased. "You get right to it, don't you?"

"I will pay you if that will speed things."

"I'm not no whore," Tandy said indignantly. "Don't spoil it by treating me as if I am."

"My apologies," Fargo said.

"That's better." She smiled and fluffed her hair. "I get off at midnight. You're welcome to stick around and walk me home if you'd like."

"I can't think of anything I'd like more," Fargo admitted. Several poker games were in progress, so he'd have something to do until then.

"I'm right pleased to hear that." Tandy rose and bent and ran a painted fingernail over the back of his hand. "I will screw your brains out."

"Promises, promises," Fargo said, and chuckled as she sashayed off. The next moment his good humor evaporated as a weasel planted himself in front of him.

"Remember me?" Harold Jaster said.

"Go annoy someone else," Fargo said.

"I've hardly said two words. And I'd like to ask you a few questions."

"No."

"About Colonel Hastings, and what he's up to. I've heard that he sent for you, special."

"Did you?"

Smirking, Jaster nodded. "He can't keep secrets from me. Not with the pittance the army pays its troops. A dollar in a palm buys me all I need to know."

"The sawbones might want more."

Jaster lost his smirk. "Let me guess. You're under orders not to speak to me."

"I just don't like you," Fargo said.

"Why are you taking this so personal? I'm only doing my job."

"Do it somewhere else."

Jaster refused to take the hint. "I've recalled where I've heard your name, by the way. You're half-famous. The best scout alive, some say."

"You are downright pitiful."

"I know you're a womanizer and fond of hard liquor and you like to gamble your nights away."

"Did you hear what I do to bastards who annoy me?"

"Surely you wouldn't strike an unarmed man?" Jaster said smugly.

Fargo was out of his chair before the muckraker could blink. He drove his fist into Jaster's big belly and Jaster folded like an accordion and squealed like a hog. Gasping for breath, he clutched at the table to keep from falling even as Fargo seized him by the front of his shirt and jerked him upright.

"Go find someone else to pester," Fargo said, and gave Jaster a shove that sent him teetering on his heels.

Most of the saloon's patrons had stopped what they were doing to stare. One man hollered, "Here, now. What's that about?"

Fargo looked at him and the man quickly turned away. To Jaster he said, "Why are you still standing there?"

The newspaperman was red in the face with anger as much as pain. "You shouldn't ought to have done that. I don't like being manhandled."

"And I don't like slugs."

"You'll regret this," Jaster said, backing away. "Just see if you don't."

"I'm trembling in my boots," Fargo said.

7

Fargo's mood improved considerably after he won over forty dollars at poker. Lady Luck smiled on him with a full house and a straight, and toward midnight she granted him four tens to beat three kings. He was raking in the pot when a warm hand fell on his shoulder and familiar perfume wreathed him.

"I'm done for the night if you're still interested," Tandy informed him.

"Am I ever," Fargo said. He filled his poke and pulled the drawstring and wrapped an arm around her waist. "Lead the way, fair lady."

"It's down the street."

Fargo pushed on the batwings and stepped out into the cool night air. He was so fascinated by her jugs that he didn't realize two men had moved from the shadows until the pair barred their way.

"What do we have here, brother?" one of them said.

Fargo looked up.

The pair was big and brawny and both wore coats, even though it was summer, and floppy hats.

"What the hell do you want?" Fargo demanded.

"I know these two," Tandy said. "They're the Bascomb brothers. They drink here all the time."

"Who cares?" Fargo gestured with his almost-empty bottle. "Out of our way."

"Listen to him," the one who had spoken before said. "He sounds right mean, don't he, Link?"

"He's not as mean as us, Gant," said the other brother.

Fargo let go of Tandy. It struck him that the pair were stone sober and not just two drunks spoiling for a fight.

"What are you two up to?" Tandy asked them. "Leave us be, you hear?"

"Out of the way, gal," Gant said. "We have work to do." And he shoved her.

Fargo's temper snapped. He swept the bottle up and around and caught Gant on the side of the head. The bottle shattered and Gant stumbled, and the next moment Link lunged at Fargo with his fists balled.

Fargo sidestepped a kick to his groin and let loose with an uppercut that rocked Link back. He followed with a looping left that spun Link halfway around. Before he could finish him, though, Gant recovered enough to throw his arms around his, pinning him.

"I've got him, brother! Wallop him good!"

Link shook his head to clear it, and waded in. "I surely will."

Fury filled Fargo. He arced his right foot between Link's legs and Link stopped cold and squawked. A surge of his arms, and Fargo was free. Whirling, he punched Gant on the jaw. It drove him back but only for a second.

"Stop this!" Tandy was shouting. "Stop it this instant, you hear?"

The brothers ignored her.

So did Fargo. His dander was up and he wasn't about to stop until he pounded them into the dirt. He countered a right cross from Gant, avoided a hasty kick by Link. Pivoting, he rammed his fist into Gant's ribs, twisted, and did the same to Link.

The brothers were huffing and cursing. They must have figured it would be easy with two against one.

Fargo was happy to disappoint them. A fist clipped his cheek and he smashed his forearm into Gant's mouth. Link swung at his neck but missed. Fargo kicked Link in the knee and, when Link doubled over, kneed him in the face.

"Stop it, all of you!" Tandy yelled.

Fargo was vaguely aware of other voices and a commotion but he didn't take his eyes off the Bascombs. To keep them from setting themselves he unleashed a flurry, hitting first one and then the other, going for the face and the gut. Their jaws were iron; they wouldn't go down that way.

He staggered Gant with a right and cocked his arm to knock him senseless when Link thrust a foot behind his leg and he tripped. He tried to regain his balance but couldn't. The next he knew, he was on his back and the bothers pounced like wolves on a buck, raining punches of their own.

Fargo blocked some but as many got through. A knee was on his chest, another across his legs. He thrust a finger into Gant's eye, and when Gant howled and jerked up off of him, he boxed Link in the ear. There was a crunch, and Link did some howling of his own as he flung himself away.

Fargo made it to his feet. He was battered and bruised and mad as hell. When Gant came at him, he stomped on Gant's toes, swiveled, and about broke his hand with a blow to Gant's head that finally felled him.

Growling like a bear, Link slammed into him.

Pain exploded in Fargo's side. Ignoring it, he landed two swift punches that knocked Link against the hitch rail. He capitalized with a sweeping smash to the jaw, their iron bones be damned.

Link fell with a thud.

In the silence that followed, Fargo swore he could hear his blood roar in his veins.

"God Almighty," someone declared. "You beat them both, mister."

Fargo felt his hat being jammed on his head, and Tandy's arm went around him.

"That was some fight, handsome. Let's get you to my place and clean you up."

Fargo winced as she pulled him down the street. His cheek was split and bleeding and his left hand throbbed.

"It's about time someone gave those two what they deserved," Tandy was saying. "They're always causing trouble one way or another."

Fargo grunted.

"Strange thing, though," Tandy said.

Fargo looked at her.

"What do you reckon they meant by having work to do? It's almost as if someone hired them to beat you up. But who would want to do that?"

"Son of a bitch," Fargo said.

8

Her room had a table and chairs and a cupboard and a bed and that was about all. A pitcher sat on the table, and Tandy half filled a basin and brought a washcloth over and dabbed at the blood.

"You'll look a sight come morning," she predicted.

Fargo let her do as she wanted. He was mulling her comment about the brothers, and what to do about it.

"Where'd you learn to fight like that?"

"I like having teeth," Fargo said.

"That's no answer. But never you mind. The important thing is that you're in one piece."

Fargo cupped her chin and kissed her.

"What was that for? I'm not done yet."

Reaching over, Fargo cupped her left breast and squeezed.

"Here now," Tandy said huskily. "You still have blood on you."

Fargo took the washcloth and dropped it on the table. Rising, he pulled her to him and she came willingly, her eyes hooded with desire.

"You don't say much, do you?"

"There's a time to talk and a time not to," Fargo said, cupping her bottom.

Tandy smiled coyly. "No, sir. You're not one for beating around the bush."

Fargo shut her up with another kiss. This time her lips parted and their tongues entwined. She groaned when he dug his fingers into her nether cheeks, and ground herself against him.

"God, I want you."

The hunger was mutual. Suddenly scooping her into his arms, Fargo carried her to the bed and eased her down. She commenced to undo her buttons while he sat and removed his spurs and his gun belt.

"I like a man who gets right to it," Tandy prattled. "Some will talk a girl to death."

"I know the type," Fargo said.

"I should have brought a bottle of my own, for after. I don't have to be back to work until noon. How about you? How much time do you have?"

Fargo was supposed to be back at the fort by two in the afternoon. "I have plenty."

"Good to hear," Tandy said. She had her dress open and was about to slide it off. Underneath, she wore a chemise and that was all.

Stretching out next to her, Fargo admired the swell of her melons and the sweep of her thighs. He grew hot all over, and felt himself stir.

"Are you just going to lie there and gander or did you have something in mind?" Tandy teased.

Fargo covered her mouth with his and her tits with his hands. She squirmed deliciously and cooed deep in her throat. For long minutes they kissed and caressed, stoking their mutual fires.

Fargo lathered her neck and nipped her lobes and pinched her nipples until they became tacks.

For her part, Tandy delved her hand between his legs and cupped and fondled his growing bulge. "Oh my," she breathed at one point. "You'll fill me to the brim."

Presently they were bare-assed, with Fargo between her legs. Her nails raked his shoulders and her mouth was everywhere.

Fargo eased his pole to her slit but didn't penetrate. Not yet. Not until she was panting and thrusting at him, mewing, "Please, please."

The bed swayed and creaked under them.

Fargo didn't care how much noise they made. His hands braced on either side, he thrust into her with mounting urgency. She was the first to explode, crying out softly, "Oh! Oh! Oh!"

Then it was his turn, and he didn't hold back. That the bed didn't break was a wonder.

Afterward, Tandy lay with her head on his shoulder and lightly ran a finger back and forth over his chest.

"That was nice. Real nice."

After the long day he'd had, all Fargo wanted was to sleep a while. Closing his eyes, he waited to drift off.

"I've been thinking about it and I remembered something that might be important," Tandy remarked.

"Mmmm?" Fargo said drowsily.

"Do you remember that gent you punched in the gut at the saloon?"

Fargo cracked an eye.

"I saw him talking to the Bascomb brothers. You don't suppose he was the one who paid them to beat on you?"

Fargo had already figured as much. "You keep bringing them up."

"I don't want you hurt, is all. You're easy on the eyes and a tiger in bed."

"How about letting the tiger get some sleep?"

"Oh. Sure. Sorry."

Fargo rolled onto his side but damned if he could fall under. He kept seeing Jaster in his mind's eye, and him punching the newspaperman in the face. He supposed he should shrug it off but it rankled.

After an hour of tossing and shifting, Fargo decided to hell with it and got up. Beside him, Tandy lightly snored. He dressed quietly in order not to wake her and slipped out.

The settlement lay still under the stars. Nearly all the buildings were dark. The saloon was still open but wouldn't be for long. Only a few horses were at the hitch rail.

Fargo poked his head over the batwings but didn't see the newspaperman. Tiredly climbing on the Ovaro, he reined up the dusty excuse for a street. He figured he might as well return to Fort Union and spend the night there. Then tomorrow he'd meet with the colonel and commence the hunt for the prospectors.

What they had done was despicable. Men who forced themselves on women ought to have their peckers cut off and shoved down their throats.

Stifling a yawn, he started past an alley between a general store and a house.

From its depths came a metallic rasp.

9

Instinctively, Fargo threw himself from the saddle even as he clawed for his Colt. He dived at the alley, not away from it. If he put the Ovaro between him and the shooter, the shooter might drop the stallion to get at him. He was in midair when the night flared with a muzzle flash and a revolver boomed.

Landing hard on his shoulder, Fargo fired. He heard a curse and the dark flamed a second time. A slug clipped the soil inches from his ear, and then boots pounded.

In a heartbeat Fargo was up and running. Staying low, he hugged the side of the general store. He thought he spied a silhouette at the far end and raised the Colt but the silhouette vanished.

He slowed as he reached the corner. Removing his hat, he peered out. Ahead was open prairie, to the right and left, the backs of buildings. He saw no movement. Nor did he hear retreating footfalls.

Fargo stuck his hat out. Instantly, a gun boomed from off to his left. He threw himself flat and saw a figure two buildings down. He fired, thumbed back the hammer, fired again.

The figure disappeared.

Fargo was about to rise when another shot thundered to his right. There were two of them, as he'd suspected there would be. Twisting, he banged off another shot of his own. Then he lay there, reloading and listening.

Shouts had broken out all over Unionville. Light brightened windows as lamps were lit. Pretty soon half the population would be out in the street, wondering what the shooting was about.

Fargo could do without a host of questions. Jamming his hat on, he returned to the Ovaro.

The bartender and three other men were in front of the saloon.

"Hey there, mister?" the barkeep called out. "What's going on?"

"Polecats," Fargo replied. Swinging onto the saddle, he rode between the two buildings to the prairie, and tapped his spurs.

He reckoned that would be the end of it, for now. But he hadn't gone fifty yards when he heard hooves drum.

Two riders were coming after him. They were reckless, doing it in the dark. Granted, the pair hadn't impressed him as having more brains than a turnip, but still.

Fargo was about to let the Ovaro have its head. But just then he came on a dry wash and changed his mind.

After riding down into it, he quickly dismounted, and shucked his Henry from the scabbard. He dashed to the top and sank to a knee.

There they were, darkling shapes. There was no moon and the pale starlight didn't help, but he could see them well enough to shoot.

Jamming the stock to his shoulder, he centered on the mass of the rider on the right, curled the hammer with his thumb, held his breath, and fired.

The shape left the horse as if slammed by an invisible fist.

The other rider was quick to return fire, several shots from a revolver. But he was shooting wild and the slugs came nowhere close. Then he hunched over his saddle horn and reined away.

The one on the ground cried out but the man on horseback didn't stop.

Fargo stayed put until the drumming faded. Rising, he cautiously approached. He heard ragged breathing and a few gasps. When he was close he pointed the Henry but he didn't use it. There was no need.

Gant was on his back, grimacing and struggling to breathe. His hands were pressed to his side, and even in the faint starlight, the wet blood glistened.

"Serves you right," Fargo said.

Gant looked up and hissed like a kicked snake. "I'm lung-shot, you son of a bitch," he said, and froth bubbled from his lips.

"If it had been daylight," Fargo said, "you'd be dead."

Gant loosed a string of obscenities that weakened him more. He lay panting and limp, his eyes pools of spite. "We reckoned we had you dead to rights from that alley."

"You should have let it be," Fargo said.

"Go to hell."

"How much did he pay you?"

Gant didn't answer.

"Suit yourself," Fargo said. "I'll ask Link when I see him."

Gant gazed into the dark in the direction his brother had gone. "My own kin and he ran out on me."

"Bastards do that."

More curses blistered the air. Gant could barely move his lips when he was done, and his chin and neck were covered with pink bubbles. "Finish me."

"Why should I?"

"I hurt," Gant said. "I hurt awful bad."

"Good."

"I wish we'd plugged you."

"Did he pay you for that too or was it your idea?"

"Go to hell."

"You first," Fargo said.

Gant's whole body shook, and he groaned. "Damn you, anyhow."

"You can take forever in pain or you can tell me what I want to know."

Gant licked his lips, or tried to. He groaned louder and said, "I hate you."

"I remember a gent who was lung-shot like you," Fargo mentioned. "It took him twelve hours."

Gant swore, and convulsed, and said weakly, "All right. All right. He paid us five dollars each to stomp you. That was all we were supposed to do."

"It was enough," Fargo said.

"You made fools of us and it made us mad. So we figured to buck you out, permanent."

"You are piss-poor at being assassins."

"Go to hell."

"Enjoy your pain." Fargo started to turn.

"Wait. You said you would if I told you, and I told you."

"That's right. I did." Fargo lowered the Henry's muzzle to Gant's forehead. "Any last words?"

"You are one mean bastard."

"I know," Fargo said, and squeezed.

10

Haylofts were better than hotels when it came to bedding down. They were usually quiet and the hay made a soft mattress.

Fargo slept in until noon, stirring only now and again as troopers went about their daily routine below.

No one bothered him. He doubted they knew he was there.

His stomach was rumbling when he sat up and stretched and gazed out the hayloft door at soldiers once again drilling on the parade ground. He scratched and put his hat on, and stood.

Bits of hay had stuck to his buckskins. He brushed them off as he moved to the ladder.

A private was putting a bridle on a sorrel and looked surprised when Fargo climbed down. "What in blazes were you doing up there, mister?"

"Counting the hay," Fargo said. He went out and over to the horse trough. Unlike the trough in town, the army kept theirs full. Placing his hat aside, he dipped his head in, then shook it and sent drops flying.

The temperature was pushing one hundred, and the water felt good dribbling down his chest and back. He put his hat back on and ambled to the sutler's. He supposed the colonel wouldn't mind if he ate at the mess but he wasn't in the mood to mingle. He bought peaches, instead.

His fingers were as good as a spoon. Squatting in front of the stable, he bit the delicious halves in half and hungrily chewed. He was about halfway through when the same orderly from the day before came hurrying over and stood at attention.

"Sir, Colonel Hastings sent me."

"Relax, boy. I'm not an officer."

"He saw you from the window and he said for me to tell you that you don't need to wait until two o'clock. You can come see him now."

"Let him know I'll be there in a bit."

"Yes, sir." The orderly did an about-face and ran back.

"Kids," Fargo said. He ate the rest of the peach halves and washed them down with the sweet syrupy juice. His fingers were sticky so he washed them in the trough, adjusted his bandanna, and skirted the parade ground and the tramping soldiers.

The orderly was behind his desk. Jumping up, he opened the colonel's door.

Hastings was over at the window, his hands clasped behind his back.

In a chair sat a grizzled beanpole wearing a hat with holes in it and clothes that hadn't been washed in a coon's age. He swiveled and studied Fargo and said, "Who's this?"

"The scout I told you about, Mr. Nestor," Colonel Hastings answered. "I want you to tell him what you told me."

"This is why your blue bellies dragged me here?" Nestor said. "Hell in a basket. You could have told him your own self."

"I'd like for him to hear it from you personally," Hastings said. "Out of the horse's mouth, as it were."

"Are you callin' me a horse?"

Hastings turned. "Were I to compare you to one, it wouldn't be the mouth. Do you follow me, Mr. Nestor?"

The beanpole in the dirty clothes scrunched his mouth and growled, "I don't like bein' insulted."

"Fortunately, one of us doesn't care what you like," Colonel Hastings said. He didn't say it in a threatening manner yet his tone spoke volumes. "You were a witness. Mr. Fargo, here, will soon put his life at risk to catch those responsible. He deserves to know all of it."

"If you say so, General," Nestor said sullenly.

"Now it is you who is being insulting," Hastings said as he moved to the desk. "Perhaps you think you can get away with it because you're a civilian and I have no jurisdiction over you. But as I just pointed out, you're a material witness to a crime over which the army has been given oversight, so it wouldn't bother me in the least to have you thrown in the stockade for a month or so if you can't be civil."

"You would, wouldn't you?"

"Do you even need to ask? And keep in mind there's a limit to my patience."

"Whatever you want," Nestor capitulated.

Fargo came around the chairs. "You saw the rape."

"Never said that, you silly jackass," Nestor replied with as much antagonism as he'd shown to Hastings.

Fargo bent and smiled. "You have a problem."

"Some folks have sunny dispositions. I can't help it if I'm not one of them."

"No," Fargo said. "Your problem is me."

"How's that again?"

"I'm not the colonel."

"In what way?"

"I don't have a stockade to throw you in. Insult me again I'll hit you so damn hard, those yellow teeth of yours will fall out."

11

Nestor drew back and gripped the chair arms. "Damn me if I don't believe you would."

"Tell him," Colonel Hastings said.

"Fine," Nestor snapped. He mumbled something, then said, "I'm an ore hound. Been prospectin' these parts since before these bluecoats came. A while back I was pannin' Antelope Creek. It's lower down than most and I never reckoned it would show color, but Tobacco Charlie found some and me and some others were workin' it that day hopin' for more."

"How many others exactly?" Hastings asked. "I don't believe you've ever said."

"Pretty near a dozen, here and there."

"Give me some names."

"There was me and Charlie and that fella from New York who came west to strike it rich, and a couple from Missouri. And no, before you ask me, I never knew their handles."

Fargo interrupted with, "I want to hear about the Apache girl."

Nestor's jaw muscles twitched. "Are you two goin' to let me tell it or not?"

Fargo gestured.

"So there we were, pannin' or workin' our slews, and suddenly down the creek a feller gives a holler and there's a ruckus and I go over to see why. These five who were workin' together had caught an Apache gal tryin' to steal one of their horses."

"How young was she?" Fargo asked.

"What's that got to do with anything? And how would I know? I can't tell ages much. Especially in redskins. They don't age like we do."

"Keep telling."

"Well, those five couldn't make up their minds what to do with her. Two of them wanted to let her go but a couple of the young ones said she ought to be punished. I heard one say he wanted to skin her alive. That younger pair was mad as hell, let me tell you. I think they were more mad because she was a redskin than anything else. They hated reds, those two."

"Go on," Fargo said when the prospector stopped.

"There ain't much left. The rest of us went back to our pannin' and whatnot and I forgot about her until along about sunset when I stopped for the day and was makin' my supper. That's when I heard it."

"Heard what?" Fargo prompted when the prospector once again fell silent.

"The sounds comin' from that tent. You know the kind. It was a ways off but I knew. They were givin' her a poke and they weren't quiet about it, neither."

"How many raped her?"

"I can't see through canvas. But only two came out of the tent when they were done. Those young ones. Right away they had a powerful argument with some of the others. The old ones were mad but those young ones sort of laughed it off at first, but then they got mad too and there was a heap of cussin'. Funny thing was, while they were spattin', that Apache girl cut the back of the tent open and slipped out."

"You saw her get away?"

"Hell no. I saw the cut later when they told us. Figured that was the end of it but here I am explainin' things for the second time in a week."

"Then as far as you know, only two of the five laid a hand on her?"

"Ain't that what I just told you? If you're not a simpleton, you're as close as they come."

Fargo let that one pass. "I need names."

"Can't help you much there," Nestor said. "I only ever talked to them a couple times. I heard the oldest one called Samuels and one of the pair who poked the gal was called Billy."

"That's all you know?"

"It's more than I cared to. In case you ain't noticed, I'm not partial to mixin' with folks. I keep to my own self and expect others to do the same." Nestor gave the colonel a pointed look.

"Think back," Fargo said. "Is there anything else that might help me? What were their clothes like? Did any of them limp or have a scar?"

"Who notices stuff like that? They were as ordinary as me. Although . . ." Nestor stopped and his brow knit.

"What?"

"Now that I think about it, that Billy did have somethin' peculiar about him."

When Nestor didn't continue, Fargo said, "This year would be nice."

"I was tryin' to remember the colors. You see, he had two different eyes. One of 'em was brown and the other was green or gray. It was the strangest damn thing."

Fargo had heard of people with mismatched eyes but he'd never actually met one. "I'm obliged."

"Don't be. I resent bein' here. I resent bein' made to help you. And I won't be the only one who resents you once word gets out." Nestor jabbed a bony finger at him. "It would serve you right if somebody slits your damn throat, helpin' a damn Apache. And especially *him*."

"That's enough," Colonel Hastings said.

"Not hardly," Nestor responded. "You're the one who told me that gal was Cuchillo Colorado's kid. This scout of yours will be lucky if he doesn't get himself killed."

12

Nestor practically bounded to the door when Colonel Hastings said he could go. As he went out he cackled and yelled back, "Good riddance to the both of you."

Hastings shook his head and sighed. "And to think. He's one of those we're here to protect."

Fargo was sorting out in his head what the prospector had told him. "If only two of the prospectors raped her, why do you want me to bring in all five?"

"We don't know it was only the two," Hastings said. "All five fled from the diggings when some Pimas let it slip who the girl was and that she had died."

"Wouldn't you?"

"That's neither here nor there. As for their guilt or innocence, it's for a court to decide. Cuchillo Colorado wants all five brought to justice and we're to accommodate him."

"About that," Fargo said.

"He'll be here in a minute, so let me make it plain," Hastings said. "Our government is counting on you to do all you can to make him happy."

"Hell."

Hastings motioned. "We've already been over why. You're saving lives by helping him."

"We could save them by shooting him."

"And have his band go on the warpath, with months and perhaps years of reprisals? No, thank you. Washington believes it's best to do it this way. Not only do we have his word that he'll stop raiding, but he'll serve as an example to other Apaches that the white man can be a friend, and that if they work with us, we can live in peace."

"That's a politician talking."

Hastings looked sheepish. "Even so, I'm under orders, and now, so are you."

There was a knock and the orderly stuck his head in. "He's here, sir."

"Show him in," Hastings said.

Fargo twisted, expecting to see Cuchillo Colorado. Instead, a monk or priest in an ankle-length robe with the hood pulled over his head entered. "What now?"

"Have a seat if you would, padre," Colonel Hastings said, smiling strangely.

The robed figured moved stiffly to a chair. He hiked at the hem of his robe as a woman might do with an ankle-length dress, then eased onto the chair as if he were wary of it breaking under his weight.

"You didn't," Fargo said to the colonel.

"I had an inspiration."

"Is that what you call it?"

The robed figure reached up with bronzed, muscular hands and pulled down the hood. "I did not want to do this," Cuchillo Colorado said.

"This just gets stupider by the minute."

"What do you mean?"

"He's joshing you," Colonel Hastings answered before Fargo could. "With that robe on, no one will know you're an Apache. You can ride into any town or settlement without causing a stir."

Cuchillo Colorado seemed more interested in Fargo's opinion. "What do you think?"

"So long as you keep your mouth shut it might work," Fargo conceded. "Just remember to let me do all the talking."

Cuchillo Colorado plucked at the robe and scowled. "I only do this to find the *pesh-klitso* men."

"The what?" Hastings said.

"The men who hunt gold," Fargo translated.

"You're welcome to requisition anything you might need from the quartermaster," Hastings offered. "I'll sign a voucher and the army will foot the bill."

Fargo was half tempted to buy a year's worth of ammunition, maybe a case of whiskey. But he said, "I don't need supplies. We can light a shuck whenever Cuchillo Colorado would like to head out."

"I want to go now."

The colonel sent the orderly to fetch the Ovaro and a mount for Cuchillo Colorado from the stable, and while they waited, he made a teepee of his hands under his chin. "I can't stress how important your mission is. If we can demonstrate to the Apaches that whites can be trusted—"

"You already brought that up," Fargo reminded him.

"—it could open a new era here in the Southwest," Colonel Hastings said, "and end decades of depredations."

Fargo could have pointed out that Apaches weren't like other tribes in that when a chief wanted something done, the rest of the tribe went along. Apaches never gave their leaders that much power. A war chief, for instance, could propose that they carry out a raid into Mexico, but only warriors who wanted to go went along. Apaches were always free to do as they pleased at any time.

Which meant that even if he did find the prospectors, and Cuchillo Colorado was true to his word and stopped killing whites for the rest of his born days, the other warriors in his band and the warriors in dozens of other bands didn't have to follow suit.

Fargo could have pointed that out. Instead he said, "If I were you, I wouldn't get my hopes up too high."

"What kind of attitude is that? Haven't you ever heard that where there's a will, there's a way?"

"I have another saying for you," Fargo said. "I just made it up myself."

"I can't wait to hear it," Colonel Hastings said dryly.

"When you dance with the devil, you get a pitchfork up the ass."

13

The first hour, Cuchillo Colorado didn't say a word. He rode with the robe hiked halfway up, revealing his knee-high moccasins.

The afternoon sun was blistering, the air was an oven. Fargo should be used to it but he sweated profusely and his throat became so dry, he resisted an urge to use the waterskin the colonel had provided.

He was grateful when twilight fell.

An arroyo offered a spot to camp for the night. They were out of the wind and their fire wouldn't be seen by unfriendly eyes.

Fargo gathered brush and kindled fledgling flames while Cuchillo Colorado sat and watched. He filled the coffeepot and put coffee on a flat rock to brew. In a bundle of rabbit fur he had enough pemmican for two and offered a piece to his companion.

Cuchillo Colorado accepted it with a grunt. He bit and chewed and said out of the blue, "You not hate me because I am Shis-Inday."

It was a statement, not a question. "I'd be a hypocrite if I did," Fargo replied. "I once lived with a Mescalero girl for a spell."

"Why you not still with her?"

"She wanted a man in her lodge. Someone to cook for. Someone to sew for. Someone to give her kids." Fargo grinned. "I just wanted to squeeze her tits."

For the first time since they met, Cuchillo Colorado smiled. "I like you, He Who Walks Many Trails. You much like Shis-Inday. Maybe we change your name. Call you White Apache."

Since they were getting along so well, Fargo decided to

come out with, "Straight tongue, Cuchillo Colorado. What do you really aim to do about these prospectors?"

The warrior's smile faded and it was a full minute before he asked, "You have children?"

"If I don't it's a miracle."

"What does that mean?"

"I've squeezed a lot of tits."

This time Cuchillo Colorado didn't smile. "I wanted sons but my wife give me a daughter. The only child we had." He added with pride, "Na-tanh fine girl."

"Her name was Corn Flower?"

Cuchillo Colorado grunted. "She try hard to please me. She learn to ride. She learn to shoot. She learn to steal horses as good as man."

Among the Apaches, Fargo knew, a skillful horse thief was rated as high if not higher than a warrior who had made a lot of kills. He said, "It was just bad luck the prospectors caught her."

"Bad luck for them."

Fargo had his answer. Not that he ever believed Cuchillo Colorado would settle for putting the rapists on trial before a white judge.

"I held her when she little, in one hand." And Cuchillo Colorado held out his, palm up. "I swing her in arms when she cry." He mimicked holding a baby and moved his arms from side to side. "She touch me, here." And he touched his own breast above his heart. "You savvy, white-eye?"

"I savvy."

It was said that Apaches were heartless. That they didn't feel emotion. That they lived for slaughter and nothing else. That they were the most violent tribe west of the Mississippi—or anywhere else, for that matter. That they delighted in torture for torture's sake, and the world would be better off if they were exterminated.

None of it was true.

Cuchillo Colorado had just proven that they cared for their families and their children as much as whites did. They felt emotion. They just didn't show it as much. To them, it was a weakness an enemy could exploit.

Yes, Apaches killed. But no more often than, say, the

41

Comanches or the Sioux. And unlike the latter, they didn't kill for the sake of killing. They didn't kill to count coup. They were raiders. They lived by stealing. And they would kill to steal what they wanted, or to defend themselves if caught.

As for the torture, it was a way of testing an enemy's courage.

That was the common threat that explained much of what they did. Their enemies. Apaches had more than most. It could be claimed, without much exaggeration, that *everyone* was their enemy.

In that regard they were unique. Where some tribes might strike alliances with others, the Apaches kept to themselves. They trusted no one. In the past, the few times they had, it cost them bitterly, and they never made that mistake again.

Cuchillo Colorado looked at Fargo and indulged in another rare smile. "Yes, I like you, white-eye. I like you and I not kill you. And I not let them kill you, too."

"Them?" Fargo said.

Cuchillo Colorado pointed.

Fargo shifted, and his gut balled into a knot.

Culebra Negro and the two warriors from the other day weren't six feet away, and Culebra Negro was pointing that Spencer at him.

14

Fargo hadn't heard a sound. Any of them could have crept up behind him and slit his throat before he could get off a shot. He didn't betray his unease. All he said was, "You again."

"Me," Culebra Negro said.

"It was no accident the first time," Fargo had deduced.

Cuchillo Colorado answered. "I asked Culebra Negro to be sure you make it to fort."

"He doesn't need to keep pointing that damn rifle at me," Fargo said.

"He does not like whites. Any whites."

Culebra Negro and the others came around the fire and hunkered on either side of Cuchillo Colorado.

"Why are they here?" Fargo asked. As if he couldn't guess.

"They my friends. They stay close."

"We protect him," Culebra Negro declared.

"That's my job," Fargo said.

"I say I like you," Cuchillo Colorado said. "I not say I trust you."

"And I don't like being shadowed."

"They not bother you. They stay close but you never see. Never know they there."

"This can only end badly," Fargo said. "You know that as well as I do."

"Corn Flower's blood cry out to me. I hear her. I do what I must."

"Goddamned politicians," Fargo said.

"Sorry?"

"I've been put in the cross hairs and I don't like it," Fargo said.

"We not kill you," Cuchillo Colorado reiterated.

"I can die just the same," Fargo said. But that wasn't what was bothering him. The ever-present prospect of becoming worm food was part and parcel of living in the West. If he wanted a safe life, he should head east of the Mississippi and take up clerking or farming.

What bothered him was that the politicians had told the army what they should do, and the army, against its better judgment, was doing it. They'd picked him because he spoke a little of the Apache tongue and knew Apache ways.

And here he was, nursemaiding a seasoned killer who was the last person on earth to need nursemaiding. With three others to deal with, besides.

Just then Cuchillo Colorado rose and the four of them went off out of earshot and squatted facing one another with their arms across their knees. They were having a palaver, Apache fashion.

Fargo sat propped against his saddle and chewed pemmican and drank coffee and thought about what lay ahead. The warmth of the fire and the low murmur of the Apaches lulled him into starting to doze off but he shook himself to stay awake.

He wasn't worried about being killed. Cuchillo Colorado needed him, and so long as he did, he was safe.

Presently the palaver broke up. Culebra Negro and the other two melted into the night and Cuchillo Colorado returned to the fire.

"Where you take us?"

Fargo was surprised he hadn't asked sooner. "The closest place to Warm Springs Canyon is San Lupe. If they went anywhere after the rape, it was there. Should take us four or five days. You know of it?"

"Small village," Cuchillo Colorado said. "Mostly Mexicans."

"It's likely they headed there for a drink and supplies, if nothing else. I'll ask around. With any luck, I'll find out where they went from there."

Cuchillo Colorado grunted. "Good plan."

"I'll do what the army wants. But I won't let you carry out your own plan."

"What do you think I do?"

"You've hoodwinked the army into finding the prospectors for you so you can hang them upside down from wagon wheels and boil their brains."

Cuchillo Colorado might as well have been sculpted from stone. Finally he said, "I not always use wagon wheels."

"Don't make it come to that."

"To what?"

"You know what the hell I mean. I'll stop you any way I can."

Cuchillo Colorado tilted his head back and gazed at the stars. "You do what you must, white-eye. I do what I must."

"Damn you," Fargo said.

15

San Lupe had been around since Spanish times. Spain had scoured the mountains for gold and silver, and San Lupe was a supply point for the miners. When Mexico declared its independence, San Lupe limped along until the Americans took over and now sold grub and picks and whatnot to a new breed of ore hounds.

Fargo had been there a couple of times. It never changed. There was a single dusty street. The buildings were mostly adobe.

Dogs and cats lounged in the heat. Hogs rooted in the dirt.

People lounged, too. Men in sombreros and serapes and women in colorful dresses.

Nearly all the signs were in Spanish, including the one above the saloon that read CANTINA.

Fargo and Cuchillo Colorado received the same treatment every newcomer would. They were stared at and studied.

The Apache had his hood well down over his face and the hem down around his feet where it should be. He kept his head low as they drew rein at the hitch rail.

It was only as Fargo was wrapping his reins that he realized it might not do to take Cuchillo Colorado in with him. The locals might wonder about a priest or monk going into a cantina. Liquor was supposed to be a vice.

Fargo decided to take the chance. He couldn't leave the warrior outside. Someone might become too nosy for their own good. "Stick close," he said, "and let me do all the talking."

It was the middle of the afternoon, early yet, and there was only the bartender and two men in sombreros playing cards and an old man half-asleep in a chair.

"Tell me you have whiskey as well as tequila and make me a happy man," Fargo said.

Portly to the point of being fat, the barkeep had slicked hair and a friendly smile. "Sí, senor." He glanced at Cuchillo Colorado. "Two glasses or a bottle?"

"A bottle, and it's just for me," Fargo thought it prudent to say. "My friend, here, only came in to keep me company."

In Spanish the bartender said to Cuchillo Colorado, "How do you do, padre? It is a pleasure to meet you." When Cuchillo Colorado didn't answer, he frowned and asked, "Is something the matter?"

That was when Fargo had an inspiration of his own. "He's taken a vow of silence."

"Senor?"

"He can't talk for a month or two. Something to do with"— Fargo had to think to remember the word—"penance, I think it is."

"Ah. Sí."

"I do all the talking and he just listens. If you ask me, his vow is a damned silly thing to do. But then he's the priest, not me."

"Show more respect for your friend, senor," the bartender said. "It is a great thing he does, giving his life to the church."

Fargo paid for the bottle and claimed a corner table. He sat where he could see the door. So did Cuchillo Colorado, his hands folded in his lap.

"That was smart to say," he said.

"Hush up," Fargo responded. "You're supposed to have taken a vow." The bottle was already open and he raised it to his mouth, and froze.

Two men had entered the cantina. Both were gringos, and might as well have "trouble" stamped on their foreheads. Their clothes were as seedy as their looks but there was nothing seedy about the pistols they wore high on their hips. They looked around and stared at the corner table.

Fargo set down the bottle and placed his right hand on the edge close to his holster.

Their spurs jingling, the pair came over. One was tall and lanky, the other short and spare of frame. It was the short one who planted himself and asked with a hint of malice, "Who might you be?"

"What's it to you, runt?" Fargo said.

The short one looked at the tall one. "Not very friendly, is he, Jenks?"

"Sure ain't, Half-Pint."

"Half-Pint?" Fargo said, and snorted.

"You think my handle is funny, mister?" Half-Pint said.

"Funny as hell."

Jenks hooked his thumb in his gun belt close to a Smith & Wesson. "You might not ought to insult my pard. I don't take kindly to him bein' insulted."

"Then he shouldn't stick his big nose where it doesn't belong," Fargo said.

"How do you know it doesn't?" Half-Pint said. "I'll ask you again. Who are you and what are you doin' in San Lupe?"

"My name is my own business," Fargo said, "and I'm being pestered by a couple of jackasses."

"You don't want to rile us," Half-Pint said.

"Everywhere I go," Fargo said, "I run into idiots."

"We're bein' paid to ask strangers what they're up to," Half-Pint said. "We do it with everybody."

"No one has shot you yet?"

"Mister, you have two choices. You can tell us and if we like what you say, we'll leave you and the friar or whatever he is be. Or you can mount up and ride out and never come back."

"There's a third choice," Fargo said.

"Not that I know of."

"What is it?" Jenks asked.

"I shoot the two of you and get on with my drinking," Fargo said, and was sure he heard a snort from Cuchillo Colorado.

"You must think you're a curly wolf," Half-Pint said in scorn.

"I think I'm a daisy," Fargo said. He was ready for one or the other to go for their hardware but Jenks surprised him.

"Hold on, Half-Pint. I have a feelin' about this one. He won't back down."

"We took the man's fifty dollars," Half-Pint said. "We have it to do."

"Since when did you get so dedicated?"

"When I give someone my word, I keep it," Half-Pint said.

"Hell. It's not like we know him. He's nothin' but an ore hound."

"Ore hound?" Fargo said.

"That interests you, does it?" Half-Pint said.

"Tell me about him," Fargo said.

"All I'll tell you is that he's been expectin' someone to come after him and it must be you."

"Why is there only one?" Fargo asked. "What happened to the other four?"

"Then you do know," Half-Pint said, and squared his shoulders. "You're goin' to get up and ride out right this minute, and no sass."

"And if I don't?" Fargo said.

"Suit yourself," Half-Pint said, and went for his six-shooter.

16

Fargo's Colt was in his hand before Half-Pint drew. He fired from the hip. The slug caught the short man in the shoulder and smashed him back. Fargo thumbed the hammer to fire again, but didn't.

A look of amazement had come over the pint-sized rooster. He looked at his shoulder and his gun arm drooped and he said, "I'll be damned." Then he melted like so much wax and lay still.

Jenks was riveted in shock. As his pard sprawled on the floor, he glanced at Fargo's smoking Colt and at Half-Pint and jerked his hands away from his waist. "No, sir," he said. "You're lightning in a bottle."

"As gun hands you would make great stable sweepers," Fargo said.

"We're not any such thing," Jenks said. "Half-Pint, there, fancies he's hell on wheels but what we are are cowpokes out of work."

"And you think it's a hoot to go around threatening folks?"

"No, sir. Like we were sayin', we were hired by an ore hound to keep an eye out for strangers. He's plumb afraid someone is goin' to come lookin' for him."

"This ore hound have a name?"

"Samuels," Jenks said. "Whether it's his first or his last he's never told us."

Cuchillo Colorado's head snapped up at the mention of the name.

"Tell me more about him," Fargo said.

"I don't know a hell of a lot," Jenks said. "A while back this Samuels and four other prospectors showed up here all agitated about somethin'. They argued, fierce-like, and one of the young ones up and shot Samuels in the leg. Then the young one and the others rode on off and left the old man here."

Fargo didn't let on that this was just the stroke of luck he'd hoped for. "How bad was he hurt?"

"Not bad at all, at first," Jenks said. "The slug went clean through. But then the leg got infected, and it's been nip and tuck. He's been weak and sickly. He paid Half-Pint and me to keep an eye out for him while he healed the rest of the way."

"He's somewhere nearby?"

"Sort of. There's an old cabin up Devil's Gulch. Been there since Spanish days. Samuels took it over and has been lyin' low since."

"Where do I find this gulch?"

"First I've got to know somethin'. Why are you after him? To kill him?"

Fargo motioned at Cuchillo Colorado. "With a priest along?"

"Oh. That's right. I can't see a padre being partial to blowin' out someone's wick. Head north out of town about five miles and you'll see the gulch to the northwest. Can't miss it."

"I'm obliged," Fargo said.

From the floor came a string of curses. "What in hell are you doin'? I come around and you're talkin' nice to the bastard who shot me?"

"I was about to get around to tendin' you," Jenks said. "And you only have yourself to blame for bein' shot. If you hadn't've drawed on this fella, he wouldn't have put lead in you."

Half-Pint did more cursing and tried to sit up but groaned and sank back down. His shirt had been stained red at the shoulder. "Damn, I hurt. How much blood have I lost?"

"A tolerable amount," Jenks said.

"As a pard you are worthless."

"What did I do? Do you want me to tend to you or not?"

"No. I want to lay here all night and bleed to death." Half-Pint demonstrated his knack for swearing again. "Help me up and out, damn it, and be quick about it. I've lost all patience with you." Glaring at Fargo, he said, "As for you, mister, this ain't over."

"How dumb are you?" Fargo said.

"Pay him no mind," Jenks said. "He doesn't know what he's sayin'."

"I sure as hell do," Half-Pint said. "I take it personal when folks put lead in me. As soon as I'm up and around, I'm comin' after this peckerwood."

"You should go back to herdin' cows," Fargo advised. "You'll live longer."

"It was luck you got me," Half-Pint said.

"Luck, hell. A turtle could outdraw you."

"First you shoot me and now you insult me. Give me my six-gun and I will try again right here and now."

"Please shut up," Jenks said. "You're an embarrassment."

Cuchillo Colorado startled Fargo by unexpectedly standing and saying, "My head hurt from so much stupid. We go now."

17

"You were supposed to keep quiet," Fargo reminded the Apache as they rode north out of San Lupe. "Now everyone will know you're not a padre."

"They not see me, only hear me," Cuchillo Colorado said. "Them not know what I be."

Fargo let it drop. No one had tried to stop them or raised a fuss over the shooting. The locals seemed to take it as a matter of course.

"We find the gulch," Cuchillo Colorado said eagerly, "we find the white-eye called Samuels."

"When we do, you're not to lay a finger on him," Fargo warned.

Cuchillo Colorado, his face hidden by the hood, didn't reply.

"Did you hear me?"

"I hear."

As they rode the ground rose. The mesquite became broken by stands of saguaro and manzanita.

That anything could grow in a land so relentlessly baked by the sun was remarkable. To survive, the plant life had to be as hardy as the animal life—or as hardy as the Apaches.

They had adapted well. They knew the habits of every type of wildlife, knew the uses of many plants. They could find water where no one else could. Where a white man couldn't venture abroad without water and supplies, the Apache needed only himself. The land provided all he needed.

Fargo imagined that Cuchillo Colorado had to be sweltering in that robe but the warrior never showed the least discomfort. When it came to showing emotion, Apaches were like the slabs of granite that thrust from the soil.

Their iron will was their most outstanding trait. When an Apache wanted to do something, he did it or he died trying.

Fargo had often thought that if there had been a hundred thousand more of them, neither the Spanish nor the Mexicans nor, now, the Americans, would ever have laid claim to any of their territory.

A piercing cry drew Fargo's gaze to a soaring hawk and its mate, pinions outstretched as they wheeled and circled in search of prey.

The only other life Fargo saw was a lizard that skittered quickly under a rock.

The dusty track they were following bore a few hoofprints but little else.

Fargo was constantly on the lookout for Culebra Negro and the other two but never caught so much as a glimpse. They were out there, though, hovering like wolves, waiting to pounce.

Eventually, the track brought them to the gulch. With its twists and turns and thick growth of dry shrub, it was an ideal place to hide.

Fargo smelled smoke before he saw the cabin. The instant he did, he drew rein.

A short stone chimney capped logs weathered by age. The gaps between them had once been packed with clay but a lot of the clay had broken off.

A mule was tied to a post, dozing in the heat. Nearby, firewood had been stacked in a lean-to. Farther up the gulch were trees, which told Fargo there must be a spring.

"You let me do the talking," Fargo reminded Cuchillo Colorado.

"This be one of those who hurt Na-tanh."

"Damn it. You gave your word."

"You not worry. I not kill him," Cuchillo Colorado said. "He can tell where others are."

"We hope."

Fargo gigged the Ovaro and approached with his hands on his Colt. He wasn't sure of the reception they'd get.

The next moment he found out. A piece of hide hanging over a window was shoved aside and a rifle barrel poked out.

"Hold it right there!" a man hollered.

Fargo drew rein. "Sure, mister. Whatever you want."

"Who are you and what are you doin' here?" the man demanded.

Fargo wasn't hankering to be shot from the saddle, so he answered, "We smelled your smoke and thought we might get something to eat."

"You thought wrong."

"How about some water for our horses, then?" Fargo requested. It wasn't unusual for travelers to stop at homesteads and farms. Usually, they were greeted hospitably.

"Take your critters and you elsewhere. You'll get nothin' from me."

"I can pay you," Fargo tried.

"I don't want your money."

"Five dollars," Fargo offered. For most people, that was a month's worth of provisions.

"No means no."

Fargo was tempted to offer ten dollars but that might seem suspicious.

"Why are you still sitting there?" the man said.

"I can't change your mind?"

"Mister, you are commencin' to rile me. Get the hell out of here before we spray you with lead."

Fargo saw no other mount than the mule. He suspected the man was bluffing about not being alone. But he held his free hand up and smiled. "If you don't want to be neighborly, we'll skedaddle."

"I ain't your damn neighbor. Go, and to hell with you."

Fargo was about to rein the Ovaro around when Cuchillo Colorado startled him again by riding past him toward the cabin.

18

"What are you doing?" Fargo said, but the Apache ignored him.

The man in the cabin had the same question. "What in hell do you think you're doin', padre?"

Cuchillo Colorado kept going.

"I will by God shoot you," the man warned. "Just see if I don't."

Cuchillo Colorado held up both hands and called out, "I come in peace."

"I don't give a damn," the man responded. "Turn around and light a shuck."

Cuchillo Colorado did no such thing. His head was bowed, as if he might be praying.

The rifle barrel had swung to cover him and Fargo was sure he heard the click of the hammer.

Fargo braced for a blast but none came. Not even when the Apache stopped ten feet from the cabin and was as perfect a target as could be.

The door was jerked open and out limped a man in his fifties or so. His clothes were as worn as the cabin. His chin was speckled with gristle. His floppy hat had holes in it and his boots were so badly scuffed, no amount of polishing would ever restore their luster. He pressed a Sharps to his shoulder and pointed it at Cuchillo Colorado. "Padre, you have your damn nerve."

Fargo gigged the stallion. He held his arms out from his sides and stopped when he came alongside Cuchillo Colorado. "I'm obliged to you for not shooting him."

"The two of you beat all," the man said. "I tell you I don't want you here and you ride right up anyway."

"We could really use some water," Fargo lied.

"I don't give a damn."

"I'm called Fargo."

"I don't give a damn about that, neither."

"Who might you be?"

"Son of a bitch! Can't you hear? My name is Samuels and this is my cabin and I won't have strangers come waltzin' in here like God Almighty."

"God loves all men," Cuchillo Colorado said.

Fargo figured he'd picked that up from a missionary. Priests and ministers were forever trying to "convert the heathens."

"Don't start on me with religion," Samuels said. "I don't believe in that bunk." He shook his Sharps. "Now, for the last goddamned time, take your asses out of here."

Fargo was about to say he'd very much like to when Cuchillo Colorado began to dismount.

"Hold on!" Samuels cried, and took aim.

Fargo was good at reading people. He had to be if he wanted to go on breathing. And he read this Samuels as the sort who was more bark than bite. The kind who gave voice to a lot of threats but didn't carry them out.

Cuchillo Colorado must have thought the same because he alighted and folded his hands in front of him in perfect imitation of a real padre. "Bless you, brother."

Samuels was dumbfounded. He stood there with his mouth hanging open, apparently unsure what to do.

"That offer of five dollars still stands," Fargo said.

"You two beat all," Samuels fumed, but lowered the Sharps. "If I let you have a drink, will you get the hell gone?"

"We will," Fargo said.

"Stay right where you are." Samuels started to go back into the cabin and then gave a start. He was staring at the Ovaro, at the waterskin hanging from Fargo's saddle. "What the hell? This is a trick."

Cuchillo Colorado sprang. With lightning speed he was on the prospector before Samuels could fire. A sweep of his arm knocked the barrel up just as the gun went off. Lunging, Cuchillo Colorado clamped a hand on Samuels's throat, hooked a foot behind his leg, and slammed him to the ground. Suddenly a knife was in Cuchillo Colorado's other hand, and he raised it on high.

Fargo was already out of the saddle. Several quick bounds and he jammed the Colt against Cuchillo Colorado's side. "No."

Cuchillo Colorado's face was still hidden by the hood. "He is one of them."

"You kill him, we might never find the others."

Samuels's eyes were trying to bulge out of his head. He managed to sputter, "You're an Apache!"

"What will it be?" Fargo said.

With great reluctance, Cuchillo Colorado let go and stepped back.

Fargo scooped up the Sharps before the prospector could think to grab it, and pointed the Colt at him. "I've been sent by the U.S. Army."

"Army?" Samuels absently repeated. He couldn't take his eyes off Cuchillo Colorado. They mirrored raw fear bordering on terror.

"You were at Warm Springs Canyon when an Apache girl named Corn Flower was raped."

Samuels finally tore his gaze from Cuchillo Colorado. "I had no part in that."

"So you say."

Rubbing his throat, Samuels sat up. "God's honest truth, mister."

"You just told me you don't believe in that bunk," Fargo reminded him.

"Then I'll swear by my mother's grave. It was Skeeter Bodine and that other one, Pratt, who did that girl wrong. I didn't want no part of it."

"How about if we go inside and you tell us everything you know."

Samuels gestured at Cuchillo Colorado. "What about him? How do I know he won't up and kill me?"

"You don't."

19

The cabin had one room with a table and two chairs and a small frame bed. The stone fireplace was black with soot, the floor caked with dust. A musty odor clung to everything.

Samuels sat at the table staring at Cuchillo Colorado. "Who is this redskin, anyhow? What's he doin' dressed in that getup?"

Fargo was leaning against the wall near the front door, his hand on his Colt. Not that he expected the prospector to try anything. It was Cuchillo Colorado he had to watch.

The Apache was over by the fireplace, the hood down around his neck, his arms folded, his features inscrutable.

"I want to know who this Injun is," Samuels insisted. "Does he work for the army, too?"

The army did employ a handful of Apaches as scouts. Their knowledge of the land was invaluable. They were also unpredictable in that the army never knew when they would take the new rifle they were given when they signed up and go back to their people and use it against the white man. "He's not a scout," Fargo said.

"None of this makes sense," Samuels spat. "What gives you the right to barge in on me? The army has no say-so in civilian things. Everyone knows that."

"Some things they do," Fargo said. "Civilians caught on Indian land. Civilians who run guns to Indians. Civilians who sell liquor to Indians." He paused. "Civilians who rape Apache women."

"I didn't rape nobody." In sudden alarm, Samuels jerked his head at Cuchillo Colorado. "Who the hell is he, damn you?"

"The father of the girl who was raped."

Samuels sat bolt upright, his eyes filling with fear. "Oh God."

"His name is Cuchillo Colorado. Maybe you've heard of him?" Fargo saw the blood drain from the prospector's face and heard his breath catch in his throat.

"This can't be happenin'!" Samuels exclaimed, and visibly quaked. "Listen," he said. "I had nothin' to do with it. Honest I didn't. I even tried to stop them."

"We want to hear all of it," Fargo said, "from the beginning."

"You won't let him hurt me?"

"I'm to take you back alive," Fargo said.

"Back where?"

"To Fort Union. You and the others."

"Good luck catchin' the ones who did it. They won't go easy, like me. They'll kill you as quick as look at you if they suspect you're after them."

"Start talking."

Samuels wiped his sleeve across his perspiring face, and swallowed. "All right. It started that mornin' the Apache girl snuck into our camp. We were at Warm Springs Canyon. Know where it is?"

Fargo nodded.

"We weren't the only ore hounds there at the time. Why that gal picked our camp, I'll never know. Unless she took a shine to Skeeter's horse. It's a dandy. I don't know much about horseflesh but I know a fine animal when I see one and that bay of his is about the finest I've ever set eyes on."

"Go on," Fargo said when the prospector didn't.

"She might have gotten away with it exceptin' she likely didn't spot Skeeter's dog."

"He has a dog too?" Fargo said.

"He did. We were off a ways, pannin' the creek, and heard it barkin' and growlin' and a god-awful ruckus. So we ran back, and she was on the ground, and that dog had her leg in its mouth." Samuels glanced nervously at Cuchillo Colorado.

"Don't stop."

"Well, no sooner did we run up than that gal pulled a knife and cut the dog's throat as slick as you please. She pushed it off and jumped up to run, but her leg was hurtin'

60

and before she could go far Skeeter and Pratt caught her and there was a tussle like you wouldn't believe."

"Don't stop," Fargo said again.

"Wilson and Ostman and me didn't do nothin'. We were too shocked by it all, I reckon. At least, I was. Her comin' out of nowhere and then killin' that dog."

"Did Skeeter and Pratt hurt her?"

"Not then, even though Skeeter was mad as hell and wanted to bust her skull. He said so. But that Pratt said he had a better idea and they hog-tied her and threw her into a tent. It took some doin', too. That gal was a scrapper." Samuels gave Cuchillo Colorado another apprehensive look.

"Let me hear the rest."

Samuels fidgeted and gestured at Cuchillo Colorado. "How about sendin' him out first? He hears it, he's liable to tear into me."

"I told you I'd protect you."

"I want to hear it from him," Samuels said. "I want his word that he won't harm me."

Cuchillo Colorado didn't speak or move.

"I mean it," Samuels said. "You can hit me, you can kick me, you can beat on me all you want, but I'm not sayin' another goddamn word unless he promises not to lay a finger on me."

"You'd take his word for it?"

"Why not? I've heard tell that if an Apache makes a promise, he keeps it."

"That they do," Fargo confirmed. As hard as it was for some whites to believe, the red man could be as honorable as anyone.

Samuels stubbornly stared at Cuchillo Colorado. "You want to hear the rest? Give me your word."

For almost half a minute Cuchillo Colorado just stood there. Then he said, "You not hurt daughter?"

"What have I been sayin'? I didn't touch her. If you want to know who did, you know what you have to do."

"I give you my word, white-eye," Cuchillo Colorado said. "I not kill you."

"I want more than that. I want your word you won't hurt me in any way."

"I not hurt you ever. How that be?"

"That's good enough for me," Samuels said.

"Good."

Cuchillo Colorado did something that Fargo found ominous. He smiled.

20

"It happened thisaway," Samuels resumed his recital. "After they'd trussed her and put her in the tent, we sat down at the fire and got to talkin' about what to do with her. Ostman and me was for lettin' her go. She was just a girl, for God's sake. But Skeeter and Pratt were for killin' her. Skeeter said as how she was red and the only good red is a dead red, and Pratt went along with him because Pratt always goes along with whatever Skeeter wants."

Fargo kept one eye on Cuchillo Colorado. So far he was acting as meek as a lamb, which was suspicious in itself.

"Skeeter said we should put it to a vote, so we all turned to Williams. He never was much good at makin' up his mind and he said he didn't know what we should do."

"And the girl was in the tent this whole time?" Fargo asked.

"Lyin' there quiet-like. I think she knew enough of our lingo to get the gist." Samuels shook his head at something he was thinking. "It would have been over then and there and we'd have let her go if Williams had voted with Ostman and me. But no. I think he was scared of Skeeter and Pratt. Especially Pratt. He's a killer, that one. You could see it in his eyes. Anyway, after the vote me and Ostman and Williams went back to our pannin'."

"And that's when Skeeter and Pratt raped her?"

"No. It didn't happen right away. They stayed by the fire, talkin' about what they were goin' to do. It's too bad there weren't more Apaches around."

"Explain," Fargo said.

"If we'd thought there were more skulkin' about, we'd have let her go right-quick. Even Williams would have agreed it was the smart thing to do. But everyone was pretty sure she was by

63

her lonesome." He paused and rubbed his chin. "Later I saw Skeeter and Pratt with him, and I figured they were tryin' to convince him to vote to do her in. Turned out there was more to it."

"How so?"

"Ostman found out they offered Williams a share of their gold if he let them have their way with her."

"By have their way you don't mean kill?"

Samuels swallowed, and nodded. "It wasn't until near suppertime that we sat back down again to hash it out. And that was when it turned ugly. Williams said he'd go along with anything Skeeter and Pratt wanted to do. Ostman and me argued that no real harm had been done except for her killin' the dog. And if word ever got out, we'd have Apaches after us for sure." He glanced at Cuchillo Colorado. "Turns out we were right."

"What did Skeeter and Pratt say to that?"

"That the girl was too pretty to waste."

"Waste?" Fargo said.

Samuels did more nodding. "That was when I caught on to what they aimed to do. I told Skeeter and Pratt it was wrong. Apache or not, the girl didn't deserve it. And do you know what they did? They laughed me to scorn. Said I was too high-minded. Said I was weak. I wanted to hit them but what could I do, me to their two?"

"And then?"

"It was after supper that they got to it. Ostman walked off in disgust. Williams went over to the creek and I saw him with his fingers in his ears. I couldn't stand to hear the doin's, so I walked off, too."

"How long did you stay away?"

"Oh, an hour or so. When I finally went back, Skeeter and Pratt were at the fire with Williams and all three were actin' like nothin' had happened. I looked in the tent, and I wish to God I hadn't."

Fargo didn't ask what he saw. Not with Cuchillo Colorado there.

Cuchillo Colorado was as impassive as a statue.

"They'd stripped her bare—" Samuels began.

"That's enough," Fargo cut in.

"No," Cuchillo Colorado said. "Say all of it. I want to hear."

Samuels gulped. "They'd had their way with her and then they must have beat her. She was bleedin' from the mouth and her face was half swollen and one or both of them had cut her . . ."

"Cut where?" Cuchillo Colorado said.

Samuels raised a finger to his chest and touched one side and then the other. "Here and here. They cut them off. I saw them lyin' on the ground and about puked."

The prospector fell silent, bowed his head, and quaked at the memories.

Fargo didn't take his eyes off Cuchillo Colorado. He half-expected him to whip a knife from the folds of the robe and plunge it into the old man's heart, but instead Cuchillo Colorado did the last thing he would have imagined.

"Thank you, white-eye," he said.

21

Samuels seemed just as surprised. "You're welcome," he said uncertainly. "I'm sorry for what they done. I have a girl of my own. Her ma died about ten years ago and she lives off in Ohio and I hardly ever see her but I care for her as much as I ever did and it would sicken me to have her die like that."

To change the subject, Fargo prompted, "Then what happened?"

"I told Skeeter and Pratt and Williams that I didn't want any more part of them. Ostman said the same. We were gettin' the hell out of there before her kin showed up." He uttered a short bark of mirth. "That rattled Skeeter, the weasel. Until that moment I don't reckon he gave any thought to what the Apaches would do to him if they caught him. Suddenly he couldn't get out of there fast enough. He said as how we should stick together, how if the Apaches did come, the five of us could hold them off better than two or three of us."

"So you packed up and ran for your lives," Fargo said.

"Packed, hell. We left our tents, the pack animals, the works. Even left our picks and shovels. I don't mind admittin' how scared I was. And the others, they got just as scared once it sunk in. We rode all that night and the next day besides. I didn't hardly sleep a wink until we got to San Lupe."

"That's where you parted company."

Samuels nodded. "It ate at me, them doin' her that way. I made the mistake of sayin' as how I aimed to go to the law. Skeeter and Pratt didn't like that. Not one little bit. They called me a turncoat to my own kind. Warned me that if I went, they'd hunt me down and bury me."

"Is that when you were shot?"

"Heard about that, did you?" Samuels said glumly. "I got

up from the table and told them they could go to hell and I was doin' as I damn well pleased, and that Skeeter cursed and pulled out his six-shooter and drilled me in the leg."

"You were lucky."

"In that he didn't shoot me in the head or the heart? I suppose. But we were in the saloon and there would have been witnesses. So he shot me in the leg and then came around and grabbed me by my shirt and said so only I could hear that if word got out what he'd done, him and Pratt would do worse things to me than they done to her."

"What about Williams and Ostman?"

"Williams didn't say a damn thing. I figured Ostman would help me, but Skeeter said that if he knew what was good for him, he'd be shed of me. And damned if he didn't up and go with the rest."

Fargo had heard enough but Samuels wasn't done.

"I figured to lay abed a few days until the bleedin' stopped and I could ride and then light a shuck for Ohio. But I came down with fever and the shakes. My leg got infected. I would have died if not for a kindly old Mexican lady who took me in and nursed me. Once I could think straight, I got to worryin'. I hired a pair of cowpokes to keep an eye out for strangers and I came here to lie low until I was all the way healed."

"Hold on," Fargo said. "How did you know about this cabin?"

"It was the old Mexican gal who told me about this place. I needed a hidey-hole, and she mentioned that no one ever came here." Samuels looked down at his left leg. "I can't hardly ride yet."

"Why not?"

"Somethin' is wrong inside. The bone is chipped or a nerve was hit. When I get on my mule, I can't go fifty feet without havin' to get off, the pain is so bad. I was hopin' that if I waited it would go away. But each day I climb on Mabel and each day it's the same."

"How are you on a wagon?"

"I wouldn't know. I ain't climbed on one since I was shot. Why?"

"We have to get you back to Fort Union."

"I've told you all you wanted. Why can't you leave me be?"

"You know better."

Samuels frowned and smacked the table in anger.

"You were planning to go to the law anyway," Fargo reminded him.

"That was before Skeeter shot me. I've had time to ponder some, and I'm not hankerin' to die over a girl I didn't even know." Samuels glanced quickly at Cuchillo Colorado. "No offense."

"Where did the others go?" Cuchillo Colorado asked. "Skeeter. Pratt. Ost-man. Williams." He said each name sharply, as if he were stabbing it.

"Ostman went to the town he's from. Williams is likely back with his family." Samuels shrugged. "The others, hell, it's anyone's guess. They could be bound for Texas, for all I know. I doubt you'll ever find them."

"As you white-eyes like to say," Cuchillo Colorado said, "care to bet?" Wheeling, he stepped to the door and gripped the latch.

"Where you off to?" Fargo asked.

"Need air," Cuchillo Colorado said. He walked out, leaving the door partway open.

Samuels exhaled in relief and said, "That went better than I thought it would."

"He gave the army his word that he wouldn't kill any of those responsible."

"He did? Well, now." Samuels smiled and leaned back. "Maybe now I can finally get a good night's sleep."

"The army will want you to testify against Skeeter and Pratt," Fargo mentioned, taking his hand off his Colt.

"I've got no problem with that. Not after the bastard put lead in me. I'll just be glad to have it over with." Chuckling, Samuels stretched, then smacked the table as he had done earlier, only this time he smacked it for joy. "Don't this beat all. Here I took me for a goner and now I can live again. I can get on with my life, leg or no leg."

"How about some whiskey to celebrate?"

"You have some?"

"In my saddlebags."

"Mister, you and me will get along right fine," Samuels said, and laughed.

Just then the leather hinges on the front door squeaked and in came Cuchillo Colorado.

"You're back quick," Fargo said.

"Didn't you like the air?" Samuels joked.

"Like air fine," Cuchillo Colorado said, moving to the fireplace and folding his arms. "Friends like air too."

"Friends?" Samuels said.

A spike of alarm caused Fargo to turn toward the door but he was already too late.

Culebra Negro was framed in the doorway, his Spencer trained on Fargo's gut. Behind him were the other two. "Move wrong, white-eye, and you die."

22

Samuels pushed to his feet, exclaiming in sudden panic, "What's this?"

"I say I not kill you," Cuchillo Colorado said. "I never say friends not kill you."

"What?"

Fargo knew that if he so much as twitched, Culebra Negro would shoot him. He was quick but not quicker than the squeeze of a trigger finger, and Culebra Negro's Spencer was cocked.

And then any chance was lost as the other two sidled inside with their own rifles leveled.

Samuels was the color of paste and opening and closing his mouth like a fish out of water. "I didn't touch her!" he bleated.

"You not stop them," Cuchillo Colorado said.

"What could I do?" Samuels said. "There were two of them and they wear pistols and I don't."

"You have rifle," Cuchillo Colorado said, with a nod at the Sharps propped against the fireplace.

"I'm no killer," Samuels said. "I've never killed a soul in my life."

The other two Apaches had continued to sidle around until they were on either side of him. They looked at Cuchillo Colorado.

The prospector was looking at Fargo, pleading with his eyes.

"Raise hands," Culebra Negro said. To stress his point, he sighted down the barrel of his Spencer at Fargo's face.

Boiling inside, Fargo did.

Culebra Negro stepped up and gouged the muzzle against Fargo's cheek. Holding the Spencer rock-steady, he reached down with his other hand and plucked the Colt from Fargo's holster. Then he stepped back until he was practically in the corner and set the Colt on the floor.

"Now, you not be foolish," Cuchillo Colorado said.

"You do this," Fargo said, "I'll report you to the army." It was a useless threat and he knew it.

"The blue coats are my enemies," Cuchillo Colorado said. "They will always be enemies."

"I was right about you all along," Fargo said. "You used them. You tricked Colonel Hastings so he'd help you find the men who raped Corn Flower."

"I trick," Cuchillo Colorado admitted.

Fargo decided to point out the mistake the Apache had made. It might buy Samuels time. "You've showed your hand too soon."

"My hand?"

"You'll never find the other four on your own."

Cuchillo Colorado smiled. "I find this one. He knows where some of the others be."

"Oh God," Samuels said.

"I'm sorry," Fargo said. If not for him, Cuchillo Colorado wouldn't have found the old man.

"All five will die," Cuchillo Colorado said. "This I have vowed. And after they are dead, I will kill many more whites. I will kill you white-eyes until you leave our land or I breathe no more."

"I knew it," Fargo said.

"You upset that I trick army and they make you help me. I know you want to stop me. I know you still might try. But I not let you." Cuchillo Colorado nodded at Culebra Negro.

Fargo started to whirl just as the back of his head exploded with pain. The room spun and his legs turned to water and the floor rushed up to meet him. He hit hard and heard a scream.

"No! Please! Dear God! Let me go!"

Fargo struggled to stay conscious. The world was a blur except for a pair of moccasins. He saw them move toward the table.

"This isn't right! I didn't touch your girl. You can't take revenge when I didn't do nothin'."

His cries seemed to come to Fargo as if from down a long

tunnel. He closed his eyes and fought a black veil that was descending.

"You were with the ones who hurt her," Cuchillo Colorado was saying. "You come to land of Shis-Inday. You drink Shis-Inday water. You eat Shis-Inday game. You look for yellow rocks that is Shis-Inday rock. And you think Shis-Inday are sheep that must do as you white-eyes say."

"I was only tryin' to make a livin'," Samuels pleaded.

"Instead you make your death," Cuchillo Colorado said.

Fargo heard another scream and made one last effort to keep from slipping into a black well.

And failed.

23

His first sensation was a buzzing sound. He felt light prickling on his face and realized something was crawling across it.

Fargo opened his eyes with a start and a bulbous fly took noisy wing. He lifted his head and groaned as fresh pain spiked him from ear to ear. His hat was on the floor. He reached for it and the pain grew worse. Grimacing, he touched his finger to the back of his head. He had a lump the size of a hen's egg.

His mouth was dry and his tongue felt as thick as his wrist. He tried to swallow three times before he could. Sliding an elbow under him, he rose high enough to look around.

The front door was wide open. Everyone was gone. So was the Sharps. His Colt still lay in the corner.

Fargo sat up and involuntarily groaned. His gut churned but it soon stopped. Grabbing his hat, he gingerly placed it on his head and slowly stood. His legs were wobbly. He took a careful step and then another and they steadied.

Bending to pick up the Colt set his head to fiercely pounding. When it stopped he moved toward the door.

More flies buzzed.

He stopped when the smell hit him. It was unmistakably that of fresh blood.

Cocking the Colt, Fargo edged out.

The mule lay by the post in a pool of drying scarlet. Its throat had been slit. A legion of flies swarmed the slash and filled the air above.

Fargo almost gasped in relief when he saw the Ovaro. It hadn't been touched. He emerged and blinked in the harsh glare of the sun. Squinting, he looked around for sign of which way the Apaches had gone and his gut churned anew but for a different reason.

It was one thing to skin an animal to eat it. Another to see a man who had been skinned alive from neck to feet after being stripped naked and staked out.

The Apaches had done other things. Unspeakable things. Things that could drive a sane person insane.

Fargo went over. The lidless slit eyes, the cavity where the nose had been, the lipless mouth, the rest that had been done. It had been a horrible way to die, he thought.

"Who's there?" the ruin rasped.

Fargo couldn't find his voice.

"Have you come back to gloat? Haven't you done enough?"

"It's me," Fargo got out.

The prospector moved his head. "Thank God! I thought they'd done you in."

Fargo moved closer. "Can I get you some water?" It was all he could think of to do.

"Finish me off," Samuels croaked.

Fargo looked at the Colt in his hand.

"Did you hear me?" Samuels could barely speak. "They left me to suffer. To take a long time dyin'."

"I'm sorry," Fargo said.

"For what? It wasn't your doin'. That Cuchillo Colorado ain't human."

"I have to know," Fargo said. "Did you tell him where the others are?"

"No. They tried and they tried to make me but I showed the bastards." Samuels trembled and gasped out, "Please. I can't take much more. Do what needs doin'."

Fargo pointed the Colt. "If it helps any, I aim to track him down if it's the last thing I ever do."

"Just so you get the mean one," Samuels said. "He did the cuttin'."

"Culebra Negro?"

"I don't know his name. He was the one who hit you." Samuels shuddered more violently. "Please. Do it. I can't take much more."

The boom of the shot echoed down the gulch.

Afterward, Fargo broke off a chair leg and used it to dig a shallow grave. He wrapped the body in a blanket, lowered it in, then gathered rocks and piled them.

The sun was close to setting when he finished. He was tired and dusty and his head still hurt like hell. The notion of spending a night in the cabin didn't appeal to him, so he mounted and headed for San Lupe.

The air cooled as the stars blossomed but inwardly Fargo simmered. He was mad at himself. He'd sensed all along that Cuchillo Colorado couldn't be trusted. Yet he'd allowed himself to be duped. He'd played right into the wily Apache's hands and now an innocent man was dead.

Although when he thought about it more, the ones he should be mad at were Skeeter Bodine and Pratt. Wherever they were he'd find them, too.

He was mulling how to go about it when feet slapped the ground, and the next instant iron hands wrapped around his leg, tore it from the stirrup, and upended him. It happened so fast, he couldn't kick free or clutch at the saddle horn.

Fargo landed on his shoulders, and rolled. He came up clawing for his Colt only to have it knocked from his hand. Steel glinted in the starlight and he grabbed at a wrist before the knife could strike. His attacker seized his other wrist and then they were nose to nose and chest to chest.

It was Culebra Negro.

The warrior hissed and exerted all his strength, and Fargo was bent back like a bow. The tip of the knife dipped at his throat. Suddenly twisting, Fargo slammed Culebra Negro down and rammed his knee onto the Apache's chest. It had no effect.

Suddenly shifting, Culebra Negro swung Fargo off. Now they were both on the ground on their sides.

The warrior sought to bury his blade in Fargo's neck, and it took all Fargo had to stop him. He rolled, or tried to, and Culebra Negro drove a knee into his ribs.

Fargo knew he must end it, and quickly, before the other

Apaches joined in. Taking a gamble, he seized Culebra Negro's knife arm in both hands and wrenched, hoping to make him drop it.

Instead, with a deft flick, the warrior switched it to his other hand, and stabbed.

24

Fargo blocked the thrust with his forearm but the tip was a whisker from piercing his throat. He pushed, kicked, and was in the clear. Rolling into a crouch, he avoided a swing at his chest. In another instant he had slid his hand into his boot and palmed his Arkansas toothpick

Culebra Negro gave a grunt of surprise. Heaving up, he slashed, and steel rang on steel. He backpedaled and Fargo went after him. In the dark the Apache did something Apaches rarely do; he stumbled.

Fargo was quick to exploit it. He cut at the warrior's knife arm, and scored. Wet drops sprayed his fingers and then Culebra Negro spun and sped into the night.

Fargo didn't go after him. Not when the others might be waiting to pounce. And there was the Ovaro to think of. He didn't want the stallion to end up like the mule.

He went to where he thought he had dropped the Colt but couldn't find it. Anxiously roving in ever-wider circles, he finally did. Only then did he slide the toothpick into its ankle sheath.

The Ovaro had gone a short way and stopped. It was looking back and waiting for him. Swinging on, he jabbed his spurs and brought it to a trot.

He didn't know what to make of the attack. Why had the Apaches spared him at the cabin only to have Culebra Negro try to kill him hours later? It made no sense.

His next step, he reasoned, was to get word to the fort. Then he would keep searching for the rest of the prospectors.

In due course the lights of San Lupe appeared. The only business still open was the cantina. Horses lined the hitch rail and from within came the clink of drinking glasses and poker chips and the murmur of voices.

Fargo added the Ovaro to those at the rail and strode in. Right away he spotted Half-Pint and Jenks playing cards. Half-Pint's shoulder was bandaged, and the glance he shot at Fargo said all there was to say.

God, Fargo needed a drink. He paid for a bottle and asked for a glass.

"Make that two, if you don't mind, senor," said a sultry someone behind him.

Fargo turned.

To say she was an eyeful wasn't enough. A mane of lustrous hair as black and bright as new ink fell to her slender waist. She had Spanish in her blood, and green eyes. High cheekbones, ruby lips, and cleavage that might aptly be described as mountainous rounded her out.

"Well, look at what I've found," Fargo said with a grin.

"I believe, senor," the vision replied, "that it was I who found you."

Fargo told the bartender to set up a second glass and filled both. He offered one to the dove and drained his in a gulp.

"*Caramba*," she teased. "You are very used to liquor, I think."

"Not me," Fargo said, and refilled his glass. "I'm a teetotaler."

She laughed and held out her hand. "I am Erendira," she introduced herself.

"That's a new handle on me," Fargo said. "What does it mean?"

"Princess."

"You could be one, as pretty as you are." Fargo swallowed only half the glass this time. The princess looked promising and he liked to make love sober.

"*Gracias*, senor. That was very kind of you," Erendira said.

"Why San Lupe?" Fargo asked.

Erendira took a small sip and wet her lips with the tip of her tongue. "I beg your pardon?"

"You could make a lot more money in Santa Fe or some other big town or city. Why pick the middle of nowhere?"

"Ah." Erendira regarded the drinkers and players of games of chance. "San Lupe is my home. I was born here, senor, and I have no desire to live anywhere else. I will die here and be buried with my *madre* and *padre*."

"It's your life," Fargo said. People who preferred to live in one place their whole lives mystified him. Why stay in one spot when there was so much more of the world just over the horizon? He'd felt that way since he could remember. It went a long way toward explaining his wanderlust.

"You sound sad for me," Erendira said. "You shouldn't be. I am happy here. Happier than I would be in a city of strangers." She ran her gaze down his body. "Some strangers, though, are easy on the eyes. This is your first visit to San Lupe, I take it? I would remember someone as handsome as you if you had been here before."

"I was in here earlier," Fargo said, and pointed at Half-Pint. "I shot that stupid son of a bitch, yonder."

"That was you?" Erendira gasped. "It has been all anyone has talked about all day." She leaned toward him and a breast brushed his arm. "Be warned, senor. The small one is very mad. He has bragged that he will repay you lead for lead."

"Not unless my back is turned," Fargo was willing to wager.

"It is said there was a priest with you. Where is he now?"

"Forget him and forget the runt and let's talk about us."

Erendira arched an eyebrow. "There is an us, senor?"

"I'd sure as hell like there to be," Fargo replied. "For an hour or so."

"Ah. That. It is all you men think about."

"If we didn't, this cantina would be empty."

Erendira laughed and said, "I will be honest with you. Women think of it too."

"At least twice a year."

"Oh, senor. We are not as bad as that." She laughed some more. "I, for instance, think of it often."

"Are you thinking of it now?"

Erendira's cheeks became pink and she said softly, "As a matter of fact, *sí*. I thought of it the moment I laid eyes on you."

"Speaking of laying," Fargo said. "Where does someone do more than think about it with you?"

79

"I live just down the street. We can go there."

"You have your own place?"

"Didn't you hear me mention my mother and father? I live with them."

"Hell," Fargo said. That was all he needed. He'd start to undress her and her father would barge in with a shotgun.

"I am a grown woman, senor. They let me do as I please."

"They let you bring men home?"

"No. But they let me bring my female friends."

Erendira reached over and cupped his chin and turned his head from side to side. "Except for the beard it will not be a problem."

"What won't?"

"Making you female, of course."

25

Of all the harebrained notions Fargo ever heard, hers was about the most ridiculous.

She wanted him to don the shawl and bonnet she had worn to work at the saloon.

"It wouldn't fool a blind person," Fargo said, holding them in either hand.

She had brought him to a small house with a fence and a woodshed. A window glowed at the front and another at the back.

"Trust me, senor. They retire early. Both are in their bedroom by now. My father is probably reading. My mother, she likes to knit. Put those on and I will sneak you inside. If they look out their window they will only see the shawl and the bonnet."

"You hope." Fargo draped the shawl over his shoulders. It barely fit. He took off his hat and gave it to her, then pulled the bonnet on by its tie strings. "I must look silly as hell."

"Keep your head down and we will do fine," Erendira said.

They went around to the back and through a gate to a porch. The steps creaked but not very loud.

Erendira opened the door and listened, then beckoned. "Not a sound," she whispered.

As if Fargo was going to give a holler. He was halfway across the kitchen when he realized he'd forgotten something. A spur jangled, and he stopped and began to take them off.

"We must hurry," Erendira advised. "My mother sometimes comes for a glass of milk."

A narrow hall brought them to a door. Fargo figured it opened into her bedroom, but no. A flight of stairs led down. "You live in the basement?" he whispered.

"Hush. And stay here." She went down the dark steps with a confidence born of familiarity. Presently a lamp flared and Fargo joined her. The room was comfortably furnished with a wide bed and a dresser with a mirror and lots of female frills.

"You go through this every time so they won't catch on?"

Erendira had moved to the bed and was turning back the quilt. "I will be honest with you. I did not ask you to wear my clothes for my parents." She folded the quilt with care. "My parents know what I do. They do not entirely approve but neither have they cast me out. The money I earn helps support us. It is a few of our neighbors who are not so open-minded. They complain if they see me bringing men in. That is why I pretend to bring in women."

Fargo doubted anyone had been fooled. "So you lied to me."

"A small lie, yes. Why do you look so bothered? I am sure people have lied to you before and about much worse."

"Lately that would be just about everyone," Fargo said.

"There. You see?" Erendira faced him with her hands on her hips and her body in a provocative pose. "Enough about falsehoods. Do you not see something that interests you more?"

Fargo didn't waste time with any more jabber. He got right to it.

Pulling her to him, he cupped a breast and squeezed even as he swooped his mouth to hers. Her lips parted and his tongue was enveloped in velvet softness. Gripping her bottom, he ground his manhood against her and felt himself rise to the occasion.

Erendira removed the bonnet and the shawl and plied his hair with her fingers. Her other hand molded his chest and his legs and slipped between them to cup him.

Fargo rose even more. He liked an aggressive female. They always made better lovers.

Suddenly scooping her up, Fargo deposited her on the bed. She smiled cattishly and crooked her leg in invitation.

"Hungry boy, are you?" she teased.

"I'm not no boy," Fargo growled, and was on her like a starved bear on honey.

It took a while to shed her clothes. Too many tiny buttons

and her chemise had six ribbons, which had to be untied. Fargo would have thought that someone in her profession would know better.

He'd long suspected that some married women wore clothes like armor and made it so hard for their husbands to undress them to discourage them from doing so.

Once he'd bared Erendira's charms, he caressed, he pinched, he sculpted her body as if it were sensual clay. She reciprocated in hungry kind.

The mutual stoking of their passion brought her to the brink. At the cusp she dug her fingernails into his shoulders and looked him in the eyes and her ruby lips parted.

"Yessssssss."

Fargo's own explosion wasn't long in coming. Slick with sweat, he coasted to a stop and rolled beside her and did something he hadn't done since he arrived at Fort Union.

He had a good night's sleep.

As usual, he was up at the crack of daybreak. Beside him, Erendira snored lightly. He quietly dressed and left the amount she had mentioned on her dresser.

Yawning and stretching, Fargo hurried out the back and across the yard to the gate. He didn't see any neighbors peering from windows.

He came to the main street and turned up it. No one was abroad yet.

A dog was scratching itself under an overhang.

He was thinking of breakfast when the quiet was broken by a slight but unmistakable sound: the metallic click of a gun hammer.

26

Fargo's years on the frontier had attuned his ears to the sounds of danger. The click of a gun hammer, the twang of a bowstring, a barely audible growl. His reflexes were nearly always instantaneous. In this case, he threw himself flat even as he drew his Colt.

A gun boomed between two buildings and lead sizzled the space he had occupied.

Fargo fired at the muzzle flash, cocked the hammer, fired again.

A figure lurched into the open. The six-gun in its good hand spat flame and lead.

A slug kicked up dirt inches from Fargo's face. He fired two swift shots, the impact jolting the figure onto its bootheels. A six-shooter thudded to the ground.

"You damned jackass," Fargo said.

Nearly dead on his feet, Half-Pint took a last tottering step. His eyes rolled up into his head so only the whites showed and he sprawled onto his side and convulsed.

Fargo stood and walked over, reloading as he went.

Up and down the street, windows and doors were opening and people were yelling back and forth.

"You couldn't let it drop, could you?" Fargo said.

Behind him someone replied, "No, he couldn't."

Fargo spun and leveled the Colt.

"Hold on, mister," Jenks exclaimed, throwing his empty hands in the air. "I'm harmless."

"You weren't here to back his play?"

"Hell no." Jenks came up and stared sorrowfully at his pard. "I spent half the night tryin' to talk him out of it.

He was no gun hand. He shouldn't have tried to draw on you that first time and he sure as hell shouldn't have tried this."

"Some people never learn," Fargo said.

"Ain't it the truth." Jenks sighed. "I finally fell asleep and woke when I heard him sneakin' down the stairs of the boardin' house. I came after him but I was too late."

"I'll pay for his burial," Fargo offered. Not that he wanted to.

"No need. Him and me were partners for goin' on six years now." Jenks looked at Fargo. "I suppose I should be mad at you but I'm not. You were only protectin' yourself." He gnawed his bottom lip, then said, "Half-Pint wanted me not to tell you but I reckon now it doesn't matter."

"Tell me what?"

"About those prospectors. Samuels and the others. They were arguin' at one point, and me and Half-Pint were curious and listened to what they were sayin'."

"And?"

"I heard one of them—Ostman, his handle was—say as how he was gettin' shed of the rest and headin' for Silver Creek."

"I'm obliged."

"Me, I'm goin' back to Texas. For cowpokes, that's as close to heaven as this life gets."

Residents of San Lupe were appearing from all over, some bundled in bulky robes, others in various stages of undress. Fingers were pointed and whispers broke out.

Fargo decided to forget about breakfast. He was in the saddle and San Lupe was a cluster of shapes on the western horizon before the morning was an hour old.

It would take five days to reach Silver Creek. A wild boomtown, it was notorious for having more houses of ill repute than anywhere except Denver. Saloons were open twenty-four hours a day, and life, as the saying went, was as cheap as a plugged nickel.

Fargo's kind of place.

Twice that day he had a sense that unseen eyes were on him. Where most would shrug it off as nerves, he trusted his instincts.

That evening, sipping coffee at his fire, he pondered whether to go on or ride back to Fort Union and tell Colonel Hastings to find someone else to put their hides at risk.

He was sure that Cuchillo Colorado and Culebra Negro and the other Apaches were out there somewhere. He was equally sure they'd shadow him to Silver Creek. They wouldn't dare enter it, though. They'd be shot on sight.

Ostman needed to be warned. If he was smart, he'd flee the territory. So long as Cuchillo Colorado was breathing, he wouldn't be safe.

Of course, to warn him, Fargo had to go there, in effect leading Cuchillo Colorado to his next victim.

"Hell," Fargo grumbled at the state of affairs.

New Mexico in the parched heat of summer was no place for amateurs. It was like riding in an oven. He didn't dare push the Ovaro too hard. As a result, the days passed much too slowly.

On the morning of the fifth day he came on a road rutted with wagon tracks that led him over a rise and down among the sprawling dens of iniquity that lined Silver Creek.

The town pulsed with violent life, like a heart gone bad. He hadn't gone a block when he heard a shot, and at the next corner two men were shoving and cursing each other.

A saloon called the Mesquite looked promising. He tied the Ovaro and strolled in. The place was only half full and he had the near end of the bar to himself. He asked for his usual bottle of Monongahela and when the gray-haired barkeep brought it, he said, "Mind if I ask you a question?"

"Askin' is free. The answer might not be," the man replied.

"Fair enough," Fargo said. "I'm looking for a prospector by the name of Ostman."

About to set the bottle down, the bartender gave him a strange look. "Are you, now?"

"I just said so. There's five dollars in it for you if you'll tell me where I can find him."

"Who might you be, if I'm not bein' too nosy?"

Fargo told him.

"Well, now. Got to admit I never counted on meetin' you face-to-face."

Fargo figured the man had heard about him somewhere.

Thanks to the newspapers, that happened now and then. "I'm just a man doing his job."

"What you are," the bartender said, reaching under the bar, "is a rotten son of a bitch." With that, he raised a scattergun and pointed the twin barrels at Fargo's chest.

27

Fargo froze. There was a saying on the frontier: buckshot meant burying. "What the hell is this?"

"As if you don't know."

A number of men at the bar had stopped talking and drinking and were staring.

"Harve," the bartender said to one of them. "Fetch the marshal. And be quick about it."

"What's going on, Poston?" Harve wanted to know.

"It's that feller from the newspaper," Poston said. "The one everyone's been talkin' about."

Harve gave Fargo a glance of disgust and ran out.

"Talking about?" Fargo said.

"As if you don't know."

Men came down the bar and from some of the tables. The looks they gave Fargo were the looks they might give a leper.

Fargo didn't know what to make of it. "Someone want to explain this to me?"

"You're a traitor to your own kind," a man with a cigar said.

"He ought to be tarred and feathered and run out on a rail," spat another.

Fargo turned to Poston. "Suppose you lower that howitzer and tell me what this is about?"

"Suppose I blow you in half for bein' a cur," Poston said. "No one here would blame me."

Several of the men nodded.

"Do it," one urged. "His kind ain't fit to live with decent folks."

A square-jawed character grabbed Fargo by the shoulder. "I say we stomp him into the floor, boys. Learn him what it means to turn against his own blood."

Fargo had had enough. He'd noticed that Poston hadn't cocked the shotgun, and none of the others had drawn their six-shooters.

"I'll start the stomping, boys," the man said.

"Hit him good, Clark," another said. "Bust him right in the mouth."

Fargo exploded into motion. He slammed his fist into Poston and wrenched the scattergun free. Spinning, he swung it like a club, catching Clark flatfooted. The stock slammed Clark's forehead and he fell back, taking several others with him.

The next moment Fargo had cocked the twin hammers and was holding the scattergun level at his waist. "Lay a hand on me again," he said. "Any of you."

Poston was clutching the bar to keep from falling. "You son of a bitch," he sputtered.

"You point a shotgun at people," Fargo said, "you shouldn't be surprised if they don't like it."

"He has a point, Poston," declared a newcomer, and a tall man with shoulders almost as broad as Fargo's own shoved through the onlookers and hooked his thumbs in his gun belt. On his right hip was a Smith & Wesson. He wore a wide-brimmed hat and a black vest. Pinned to the vest was a tin star.

"He hit me, Marshal," Poston rasped. "Arrest him and I'll press charges."

"I saw the whole thing as I came in," the lawman said. "He acted in self-defense."

"So? You know what he's up to."

"That's no cause to shoot him."

"Like hell," a pudgy man growled. "He sticks around, you'll be buryin' the bastard."

"What the hell is this all about?" Fargo asked.

The lawman tilted his head. His brown eyes were lit with amusement more than anything else. Holding out a hand, he said, "I'll take that scattergun if you don't mind. And even if you do."

Fargo pointed it at the floor, let down the hammers, and gave it over. "Now will you explain it to me?"

"You really don't know?"

"If I did I wouldn't ask."

"I'm Marshal Adams, by the way," the lawman said. He tossed the shotgun at Poston, who barely caught it. "Put that behind the bar and keep it there. You pull it without cause again and I'll throw you in jail."

"Damn it, Adams," Poston said. "How can you take his side?"

"See this?" Marshal Adams said, and tapped the tin star. "The only side I take is the law's. And the scout, here, isn't a lawbreaker. He's doing it for the army."

"Army, hell," Poston said. "That don't make it right."

"Sure doesn't," Clark echoed, and others nodded in agreement.

Marshal Adams looked from man to man. "Let me make it clear. Spread the word. Anyone lays a finger on him, they answer to me." He frowned. "To be honest, I don't like it, either. But the law's the law."

"It's a fine how do you do," Clark complained, "when we have to kowtow to a damned Injun lover."

"He's just doing his job," Marshal Adams reiterated. He crooked a finger at Fargo. "You'd best come with me." He motioned, and the men blocking his way moved aside.

Glares of spite followed Fargo out. One man over at a table raised a bottle to throw it but the lawman glanced sharply at him and he lowered it again. Two men at the batwings weren't disposed to move until Marshal Adams placed his hand on his Smith & Wesson. Then they reluctantly backed off.

Once on the boardwalk, the lawman remarked, "Thank your lucky stars, mister. It wouldn't have taken much to set them off."

"What riled them in the first place?" Fargo wanted to know.

"You haven't figured it out yet? Then let me enlighten you. Right about now, you're the most hated gent in the territory."

28

The marshal's office was in the middle of town. Small and spartan, it had a desk and chairs and a cell barely big enough to hold three prisoners.

Marshal Adams sat with his boots propped on the desk and laced his fingers on his chest. "Have a seat."

"You said you'd explain."

"And I will." Adams moved several circulars. Under them was a newspaper. He pulled it out, unfolded it, and said, "I take it you haven't seen this yet? It's the latest Santa Fe *Guardian*. The stage brought a stack yesterday."

Fargo held his hand out to take it.

"How about I read the headline to you?"

Puzzled, Fargo said, "Suit yourself."

Adams cleared his throat. "'Army agrees to help Apaches hunt white men.'"

"What the hell?"

"There's a lot more," Adams said, and went on reading. "'Your correspondent has learned of secret negotiations between the United States Army and the renegade Apache killer known as Cuchillo Colorado.'"

"Correspondent?" Fargo interrupted.

Adams tapped the paper. "Says here his name is Harold Jaster."

"Son of a bitch."

The lawman resumed. "'The army refuses to confirm the report but we have it on reliable authority that a scout by the name of Skye Fargo is at this very moment engaged in hunting down five prospectors who were involved in an incident at Warm Springs Canyon. And as incredible as it is to believe, he is doing it at the behest of the most vicious Apache on the frontier.'"

Fury boiled in Fargo's veins. This was Jaster's way of getting back at him. By now the newspaper would be all over the territory.

Adams had gone on. "'What can these prospectors have done that the army would form so unholy an alliance?'" The lawman looked up and grinned. "This Jaster sure has a way with words, doesn't he?"

"He's a worm," Fargo said.

Adams chuckled and continued to read. "'Your correspondent has learned that an Apache tried to steal their horses. They caught the devil in the act, and the Apache later died. Since the horse thief was a member of Cuchillo Colorado's band, the renegade has demanded that the prospectors be brought to account, and incredibly, the army has capitulated and sent their man Fargo to do the dirty work.'"

"Why, that—" Fargo said, and didn't finish.

"'This reporter has learned that the army has gone so far as to permit Cuchillo Colorado to oversee the hunt. Now we ask you, since when is it proper for the Unites States government to enter into secret negotiations with a sworn renegade? Since when is it right that men who were only protecting their property be answerable to a red savage? And since when is it decent for a white man to hunt down his own kind?'"

"Damn him," Fargo said.

Marshal Adams gave the newspaper a slight shake. "Not an hour after this hit town, everyone had heard about it."

"I wonder why," Fargo said dryly.

"This Jaster makes you sound like the scum of the earth."

"It's his way of getting back at me for slugging him."

"Is what he wrote true? Are you helping Cuchillo Colorado hunt down some prospectors for the army?"

"The Apache who tried to steal their horses was his daughter. They raped her and she died."

"Well, now," Adams said.

"He gave his word that if the army helped him, he'd stop killing whites."

"Jaster doesn't mention any of that."

"He wouldn't."

Marshal Adams set the newspaper on the desk. "You know what he's done, don't you? He's painted a target on your back for everyone who hates redskins. And there are a lot of them out there."

"Where do you stand?"

"Silver Creek is about as wild and woolly as a town gets. I have to keep a lid on things, and I do that by being fair. Ask anyone and they'll tell you I go by the letter of the law."

"So I can count on you for help?"

"About that." The marshal gazed out the front window at the pedestrians and riders and wagons passing on the busy street. "You saw how it was at the saloon. A lot of folks would hold it against me if I were to lend you a hand finding these hombres. I'll do what I can to protect you but I won't help in your hunt."

"You call that fair?"

"I call that smart," Marshal Adams said. "I live with these people day in and day out. I can't afford the ill will."

"You sound like a politician."

"A good lawman has to be. Which is why when you step out that door, you're on your own. Oh, I'll come running if there's trouble. But by then it will probably be too late."

Fargo stood. "Thanks for nothing."

"I showed you the newspaper, didn't I? Now you know what you're up against."

Fargo stepped to the door. "Do you know a man by the name of Ostman? Can you tell me that much, at least?"

"They would know you got it from me."

"Then he is here. I'll find him on my own." Fargo opened the door.

"Good luck," Marshal Adams said. "And remember that target on your back."

29

Word was spreading.

No sooner did Fargo start down the street than a man at the next corner pointed at him and said something to two others. All three glared as he strode by and one fingered the hilt of a knife.

By nightfall, Fargo reckoned, everyone in Silver Creek would know. Word was bound to reach Ostman and he would lie low. Rooting him out would be next to impossible.

Fargo hadn't counted on any of this. He'd agreed to do as the army requested but that was before Cuchillo Colorado broke his word.

The way he saw it, he should ride to Fort Union and inform Colonel Hastings that he was done with the whole mess.

But there was the not so little matter of Samuels. The old prospector was dead because he'd led Cuchillo Colorado right to him.

Cuchillo Colorado had used him, and Fargo resented it. Duping the army was one thing. Duping *him* made it personal.

The way Fargo saw it, if he kept after the prospectors, sooner or later he would run into Cuchillo Colorado and Culebra Negro again and he could repay them for the bump on his head at the cabin and having to bury an innocent man.

So instead of heading for Fort Union, as anyone with a lick of common sense would do, Fargo bent his boots to the next saloon he came to and asked the bartender if he knew an ore hound by the name of Ostman. The bartender told him to go shove a bowie up his ass.

Fargo did the same at the next two saloons and was debating going into a bordello to inquire when he noticed a store across the way with a large sign that read MINER'S SUPPLY.

He made a beeline. Miners and prospectors used a lot of the same tools and equipment.

Pans and picks and a sluice were on display in the window. Inside, the shelves were lined with everything anyone in the ore profession could ever use.

A balding middle-aged man in an apron was scribbling in a ledger when Fargo came to the counter.

"Yes? May I help you?"

"Ostman," Fargo said. "Where can I find him?"

"Archibald Ostman?" the man said. He raised his head and gave a mild start.

"You know about me from the newspaper, don't you?"

The man didn't seem to know what to say.

"I'm on official army business," Fargo tried, "and I need to find Ostman right away."

"Do you, indeed?" The man sniffed as if he'd caught a foul reek. "I don't know anyone by that name."

"Liar."

"I won't be insulted in my own establishment," the man said. "I'll thank you to leave."

"Not until you tell me where Ostman is."

"What will you do if I refuse? I warn you that if you lay a finger on me, I'll have you arrested, army or no army."

"All I want is to talk to him."

"A likely story."

Fargo smothered a burst of anger. "How about this? You get word to him that I'd like to talk. Have him send word to me when and where to meet."

"As if he would," the man said. "The newspaper made it quite plain what you're up to."

"Tell him Samuels is dead."

"Who?"

"He'll know." Fargo turned. "I'll be out in front of the marshal's office, waiting."

And that was where he planted himself. He sat on the

boardwalk and poked in the dust of the street with a stick and drew a lot of stares and glares.

He'd been at it about half an hour when boots appeared near his stick. He peered up from under his hat brim. "Grab a stick and join in."

"Are you waiting for me?" Marshal Adams asked.

"No."

"Then what do you think you're doing?"

Fargo tapped the stick on one of his doodles. "I ran out of curlicues and started on shapes. They call this a triangle. That other is a square."

"Are you loco?"

"I'm waiting for Ostman."

"Here?"

"Can you think of a safer place? The good citizens of Silver Creek aren't likely to string me up in front of your office."

"Has anyone ever told you that you're a devious son of a bitch?"

"Mostly I keep it a secret."

"I should arrest you."

"For what? Drawing in the dirt?"

"Damn it, Fargo. Everyone will think I helped you."

"No, they won't. Ostman will set them straight."

"Not if you've drug him off to Fort Union."

"I'm not taking him anywhere."

Adams's eyebrows pinched together. "What game are you playing?"

"It's called catch Cuchillo Colorado and blow the bastard's brains out."

"Damn me if I don't think you're serious."

"I am."

"But you're supposed to be working with him. The newspaper said so."

"He broke his word to the government, and used me, besides."

"You don't say." The lawman surprised Fargo by sitting down beside him. "This puts a whole new slant on things. Why didn't you tell me this earlier?"

"You were too busy being fair."

Adams colored slightly and began, "That's not . . ."

"Fair?" Fargo finished.

They both grinned, and the marshal looked past him and abruptly sobered. "I'll be damned."

"What now?" Fargo asked, looking up.

"See that gangly gent in the stovepipe hat?"

"I do."

"That there is Archibald Ostman."

30

Fargo rose and waited with his arms folded.

Ostman had the look of a wary bird ready to take flight. His eyes darted every which way and one hand was on a revolver tucked under his belt. He hadn't shaved in a few days and his skin and his clothes were soiled. His boots were so scuffed, no amount of polish would restore them. He regarded Fargo with suspicion. "Kennart over to the mining emporium said you wanted to see me."

"You know who I am?"

Ostman gave a curt nod. "I read about you in the newspaper."

"Do you believe in fairy tales, too?"

"Eh?" Ostman said.

Marshal Adams broke in with, "It's not what you think, Arch. He's not here to take you in."

"I want to know about Samuels," Ostman said. "Him and me were friends. Good friends. How did he die?"

"I'll get to that," Fargo said. "Pick a place to eat while we talk."

"I'm not hungry."

"I am. I haven't had a bite all day."

"There's Maude's around the corner," Marshal Adams said. "She has some of the best food anywhere."

"I suppose it can't hurt," Ostman said, although he didn't sound happy.

The lawman escorted them to the restaurant, a homey place with flowered curtains and tables with tablecloths and high-backed chairs. He claimed one for himself.

"You're hungry too?" Fargo said.

"I want to hear it," Adams said.

The stout woman who came to take their order had a kindly smile and a motherly look. If she'd heard about Fargo, she gave no sign.

Ostman had been studying the menu. "Who's paying for this?"

"I will," Fargo offered.

"In that case I'll have steak with all the trimmings."

"Make that two," Fargo told Maude.

"Coffee and a biscuit for me," Marshal Adams said. "And leave the pot."

Ostman leaned back, his hand still on his revolver. "I'm ready to hear you out."

Fargo told him everything. About being sent for by the army. About the arrangement with Cuchillo Colorado. About Samuels's grisly death.

"Sweet Jesus," the prospector said, aghast. "He didn't deserve that. He had no hand in the girl. Neither did me or that worthless Williams."

"Cuchillo Colorado doesn't care who did and who didn't," Fargo said. "He wants all of you dead. That's part of the reason I came looking for you. To warn you."

"I'm safe so long as I stay in town. But what's the other part?"

"Where can I find Williams and those other two? Skeeter and Pratt?"

"I don't know as I should say."

"Be reasonable, Arch," Marshal Adams said. "He came all this way not knowing about the newspaper story. He thought he was doing you a favor. You'd have gone off prospecting and Cuchillo Colorado would have gotten his hands on you."

Just then the food arrived.

Fargo's stomach rumbled at the aroma. The steak was an inch thick and sizzling with fat, the potatoes were smothered in melted butter, the bread was warm and soft, the peas delicious. He ate with relish.

Ostman was halfway through when he stopped chewing to say, "All right. I've made up my mind. I'll tell you where they are. But if Skeeter and Pratt have read that paper, they're liable to throw down on you the moment they set eyes on you."

"I'll take that chance." Fargo didn't reveal he had a special reason for wanting to find those two. "Tell me a little about them."

"They're young and reckless. If they weren't prospectors they'd make great owlhoots. They think they know it all, but then, who doesn't at their age?"

"And they like to rape women."

"Just that Apache gal, that I know of," Ostman said. "Skeeter can't abide Injuns. They killed his ma and pa when he was ten or eleven, and he's nursed a powerful hate ever since."

"And Pratt?"

"He does whatever Skeeter does. Sort of his shadow, you might say."

"What about Williams?"

"He's useless. Has no backbone whatsoever. Oh, he did his share of the work and never complained, mind you. But he has no more of a spine than a sponge. He wouldn't stick up for that girl and he didn't stick up for Samuels when Skeeter shot him."

"Why didn't you stay with Samuels?"

"Skeeter was waving that six-shooter of his at me, saying as how he had half a mind to shoot me, too, since I was against hurting that gal from the start. I hated leaving Samuels but I skedaddled."

"Where do I find them?"

"Ever hear of Titusville?"

Fargo nodded. It was a small town about three days' ride. A farming community, he seemed to recollect, settled by Quakers or some such from back east.

"That's where you'll find—" Ostman stopped and gazed past Fargo toward the entrance. "There's something you don't see every day."

Before Fargo could turn, Marshal Adams, who was facing in that direction, remarked, "Where in the world did that priest come from?"

31

Surely not, Fargo thought, as he spun in his chair.

Everyone in the restaurant had stopped eating to stare at the padre.

Maude happened to be near the door and moved toward the figure in the familiar robe, who stood with his hands up his sleeves. "May I help you?"

Fargo opened his mouth to shout a warning but it was too late.

Cuchillo Colorado's left hand streaked out holding a long-bladed knife. He slashed Maude across the throat and scarlet sprayed. In the selfsame instant his right hand appeared with a revolver already cocked. He pointed it at Archibald Ostman and fired. The slug caught the prospector in the face and flipped him and his chair back.

It all happened so fast that Maude and Ostman were crumpling to the floor before anyone else galvanized into motion.

Fargo and Marshal Adams both heaved out of their chairs, clawing for their hardware as they rose.

Cuchillo Colorado was quicker. Whirling, he leaped at the window and crashed through it in a spectacular shower of shards and slivers.

Screams and wails filled the restaurant.

Fargo flew to the door, pushing a man who rose in his path. The man squawked and cursed, and then Fargo was out in the bright glare of the sun.

Passersby had stopped in consternation when the window exploded. An old woman was on her hands and knees, wailing.

A man in a bowler pointed down the street and said, "A monk hit her and lit out."

Fargo gave chase. He marveled at the Apache's audacity in venturing into the heart of town. Then again, Apaches were nothing if not fearless when on the warpath. And this was more than a warpath to Cuchillo Colorado. This was a personal vendetta.

People had stopped and were staring in the direction he was running. One of them heard him pound up and said, "A priest just went thataway. What did he do that you're after him?"

Fargo didn't answer. At the next intersection he stopped, seeking some sign of which way Cuchillo Colorado had gone. Pedestrians were going about their usual routines, undisturbed. He asked several if they had seen a man in a robe go by and they either shook their heads or told him no.

It was as if the Apache had reached this point and vanished into thin air.

Acting on the assumption that Cuchillo Colorado would want to get clear of Silver Creek as quickly as possible, Fargo was about to continue to the west when boots pounded and Marshal Adams overtook him.

"Where is he?" the lawman asked breathlessly. He was holding his revolver and was slick with sweat from running.

"I lost him," Fargo said. "But I think he went this way." He broke into a jog.

Adams huffed and kept pace, saying, "Archibald Ostman is dead."

"Figured as much."

"That was him, wasn't it? Cuchillo Colorado?"

Fargo was trying to concentrate on the people and riders ahead. None showed any sign that anything out of the normal was taking place.

"I can't hardly believe it," the lawman marveled. "To come into town like that and shoot Ostman right in front of us."

"He's a Jicarilla Apache."

"Even so," Marshal Adams said.

Fargo saw an old man in a chair, a corncob pipe stuck between his lips, and slowed to ask, "Did you see a man in a robe go by?"

"Sure didn't, sonny," the old-timer said.

Fargo went to the end of the next block and stopped. Only

one remained. Beyond spread open country, with nary a man in a robe in sight. "We've lost him."

"How is that possible?"

"Maybe he ducked into a doorway somewhere, or an alley," Fargo speculated. "Or he shed the robe for some other clothes."

"I don't believe this," Adams said again. "In broad daylight."

Fargo figured the lawman was upset about Ostman, but no.

"I'll be a laughingstock. They'll say he waltzed in under my nose and got away as slick as could be. I'll be lucky to hold on to my job."

Fargo didn't say anything.

"I'm organizing a posse," Marshal Adams declared. "I take it I can count on you to go along?"

"No."

In the act of turning, Adams stopped. "Why the hell not? You're to blame as much as that Apache."

"I must have missed that part."

"You led him here," Adams said. "He followed you from San Lupe, I bet. And then you went and met with Ostman." He scowled. "Hell, if I didn't know better, I'd swear the two of you were in cahoots."

Fargo almost slugged him.

"Give me one good reason why you won't come with my posse."

"How long was Cuchillo Colorado standing there before you noticed him? Did you see him come in?"

"No. I happened to look up and there he was. What does that have to do with it?"

"He might have heard Ostman mention Titusville."

Adams blinked a couple of times. "And that's where Williams or those other two might be. Ostman never said which."

"That's why I can't go with you."

"You aim to fan the breeze and warn them?"

Fargo nodded.

"I reckon I'd want to do the same if I was in your boots. You've led Cuchillo Colorado to two of them now. If you don't get there in time, he'll have three or more to thank you for."

Fargo didn't like having his nose rubbed in it but Adams wasn't done.

"That Apache has played you for a fool. The way things are going, you're liable to end up a bigger laughingstock than me."

32

It was true, and it ate at Fargo like acid as he rode hell-bent for leather for Titusville.

Cuchillo Colorado hadn't just played him for a fool. The wily Apache had hoodwinked the army, too. So what if political pressure was brought to bear to persuade the military to go along? Men like Colonel Hastings weren't idiots. They knew that to a warrior like Cuchillo Colorado, giving his word to the white man was no word at all. Whites were his enemies. His whole life long, Cuchillo Colorado had been their implacable foe. No one with a shred of common sense would expect him to change.

The only way to stop Cuchillo Colorado from killing whites was to kill him.

And from here on out, any chance he got, Fargo would take it.

He would have liked to ride the entire night through but he had the Ovaro to think of.

As he lay listening to the wails of coyotes, he wondered if he was making a mistake. Maybe Cuchillo Colorado *had* heard Ostman and was even now headed for Titusville. Or maybe Cuchillo Colorado hadn't, and was shadowing him once more, counting on him to lead them to the next prospector?

Once again, Fargo didn't have much choice but to keep going. He hated it. He hated the whole mess.

Sleep came but it was fitful. He woke several times at slight sounds even though he knew the Apaches wouldn't kill him until he'd served his purpose.

Sunrise found him in the saddle.

He recollected a well-known general who once said that only an Apache could adapt to the harsh terrain. But the general had it backward. The land molded the people, not the other way around. The Apaches were made hard by their surroundings.

The second night was a repeat of the first. The same with the second day.

If Cuchillo Colorado and his friends were out there, they were staying well hid.

Along about the middle of the third morning, a splash of green broke the monotony of brown. Like an oasis, the long valley that unfolded before him was rich with life. Tilled fields stretched for miles. Cornstalks had sprouted, pushing their tassels skyward.

Titusville was named after the first farmer who settled there. Now over five hundred souls strong, in another ten years it might become one of the biggest towns in the territory. Provided the Apaches left it alone.

So far, strangely, they hadn't harmed a single soul. Livestock, however, disappeared all the time. More than from any other settlement.

Fargo suspected that was why the Apaches left the inhabitants alone. Why kill a golden goose? He was thinking that as he rode down the main street.

Unlike a lot of settlements, Titusville wasn't dusty and dingy and ready to blow away with the next strong wind. Many of the buildings were brick, the windows sparkled, the boardwalks had been swept. It was about the cleanest town he ever saw.

The people were about the friendliest, too. Men in straw hats and overalls nodded in greeting, and women in bonnets and long dresses smiled.

But there wasn't a saloon to be seen.

Fargo drew rein at a hitch rail in front of a feed and grain and dismounted. He was stretching and surveying the populace when a heavyset man dressed no differently from anyone else but with a badge pinned to a suspender ambled up.

"This is your lucky day, stranger."

"I could use one," Fargo said.

"I'm Marshal Heigstrom. Pietor to my friends. I'm the law here. Often I'm out at my farm but I happened to have come in today and saw you ride up."

Fargo looked at the man's waist. "Forget your gun belt?"

"I don't wear a firearm," Heigstrom said with a grin. "I never need one."

"What planet am I on again?"

The lawman laughed. "We are scoffed at a lot. But we are peaceful folk, and we won't be tainted by the vices of the outside world."

"Defending yourself is a vice?"

"Defend ourselves from whom? We don't have a bank, and hard liquor is outlawed. What do we have that would draw those who prey on their fellow man? Cows?" And he laughed louder.

"What about the Apaches?"

"They're fond of our horses and our cows and leave us be."

"You don't mind having your animals stolen?"

"Mind?" Marshal Heigstrom chuckled. "We encourage it by having more than we need."

"How's that again?"

"We leave our barns unbarred at night so the Indians may sneak in and help themselves." Heigstrom winked. "The secret to living with wolves is to keep them well fed."

"I'll be damned."

"I hope not." Heigstrom pointed down the street. "Would you like to visit our church?"

"I'd like to talk about Cuchillo Colorado."

Heigstrom's smile froze on his face.

"I take it you've heard of him?" Fargo said. "He's on his way here, and he won't be content to steal a horse or a cow. He's out to kill someone."

"You know this for a fact?"

"I do."

"And who might you be, if you don't mind my asking?"

Fargo told him.

"Ah," Heigstrom said. "I suspected as much." He held out

his hand. "I'll take your revolver and that rifle I see on your saddle."

"What the hell for?" Fargo said in surprise.

"It should be obvious," Heigstrom said. "I'm placing you under arrest."

33

Fargo didn't like that eight or nine passersby had stopped to stare. Most were men and might jump in if he raised a hand against their peace officer. "I'd like to know why," he stalled.

"You were in the newspaper," Heigstrom said. "We know what you're up to."

"I'm doing it for the army."

"We don't care who you are doing it for. We protect our own."

"Then one of them is here," Fargo said. "Give me a name."

"Your revolver and your rifle," Heigstrom repeated. "We can discuss this more at the jail."

Fargo was half tempted to vault onto the Ovaro and light a shuck. "What's the charge you've trumped up?"

"Here now. I'm being reasonable. I'm taking you in for disturbing the peace."

"I haven't done a damn thing."

"You intend to." Heigstrom wriggled his fingers. "All I want to do is stop you from causing trouble while we have a talk."

"The army won't like this."

"What will they do? They can't interfere in civilian matters. They might send someone to lecture us on our bad manners but that will be all." Heigstrom chortled.

"Just so all you want to do is talk," Fargo said, and reluctantly handed his Colt over. If he played his cards right, he might learn what he needed to know. Turning, he slid the Henry from the saddle scabbard.

"I thank you. Now, if you'll follow me."

More of the citizenry had stopped to watch.

Fargo grew uncomfortable under their hostile stares.

There wasn't a friendly face in the bunch.

Heigstrom noticed, too, and remarked, "You can't blame them for not liking you. You're here after one of us and we protect our own."

"It's Williams, isn't it?"

"I refuse to say."

The "jail" turned out to be a room with no cell at the rear of a farm implement store. The customers gave Fargo the same hard glares as the people in the street.

"How is it everybody knows who I am?" Fargo asked. It seemed unlikely that everyone read the damn newspaper.

"We had a town meeting about you," Heigstrom revealed. "About what to do if you showed up."

"Hell."

"You sure do curse a lot."

"I haven't even started yet."

Heigstrom made a clucking sound. "Haven't you heard that right speech shows a right mind?"

That was a new one on Fargo and he said so.

"We take pride in living by our principles. The rest of the world can wallow in sin if it wants, but not us."

"Yet one of you is a gold hound."

"You're suggesting he is greedy? Not so. He helps work a farm, Mr. Fargo. Prospecting is for him what you might call recreation. If he ever struck it rich, he would share his wealth with the rest of us."

"Sure he would."

"You're too cynical by half." Heigstrom indicated a chair. "Have a seat." He placed the Colt and the Henry on his desk and sat. "The only reason he took it up to begin with was because a friend of the family asked if he was interested in going along."

"His friend being?"

"I suppose it won't hurt to tell you that much," Heigstrom said. "The family friend is Archibald Ostman."

"Was," Fargo said.

"You don't mean—?"

Fargo nodded. "Cuchillo Colorado killed him. And if he hasn't shown up here yet, he will soon."

"He knows about Williams?" Heigstrom blurted.

"So I was right," Fargo said.

Heigstrom puckered his brow and drummed his fingers on the desk. "This is bad. Isaiah Williams is as decent as the year is long. He had no hand in what those other two did to that poor Apache girl. He assured us so at the town meeting."

"Cuchillo Colorado doesn't care if he did or he didn't. He wants all of them dead. So far he's killed Samuels and Ostman."

"The Williams family must be warned."

"I agree," Fargo said, intending to go with the lawman whether Heigstrom wanted him to or not.

Just then there was a knock at the door.

"Who is it?" the marshal called out.

The door opened, framing a huge man in overalls and a straw hat. Behind him were others.

Heigstrom acted surprised. "Morganstern? What do you want? I'm afraid I'm busy at the moment."

"We've come for him," the huge farmer rumbled, and pointed a thick finger at Fargo.

"I beg your pardon?"

"We agreed at the town meeting that we wouldn't let him take him, remember?" Morganstern said.

"Of course I do. I have the matter well in hand. There's no need for you to interfere."

"We think differently."

"We?" Heigstrom said, gazing nervously past the big farmer at the others.

"Ten or twelve of us," Morganstern said. "We just talked it over and think the best thing to do would be to be rid of the scout."

"Rid of him how?"

"We aim to tar and feather him and ride him out of town on a rail."

34

Fargo had nearly been tarred and feathered once. It wasn't an experience he cared to repeat. "Like hell you will," he said, and started to come out of his chair.

"Stay seated," Marshal Heigstrom said. "I'll handle this." Rising, he came around the desk. "There will be no tar and feathering, Morg."

"We did it to that drummer who was selling whiskey," Morganstern said.

"He wouldn't stop trying even after I told him to leave."

"And to that corset salesman who got fresh with Mrs. Parnsickle."

"He had no manners and was a lecher, besides. And to get fresh with her, of all people. She's over forty and built like a cow."

Morganstern pointed at Fargo again. "What this one wants to do is worse. We strip him and cover him with hot tar and chicken feathers and we'll never see him around here again."

"You don't know that," Heigstrom said. "He strikes me as harder than most."

"I won't be tarred and feathered," Fargo declared.

"You don't get to say, mister," Morganstern said. "Riding in here all high-and-mighty, looking for one of us who never did anybody any harm."

"No, he didn't rape the Apache girl," Fargo said, "but he didn't try to stop it, either."

"That's not how we do," Morganstern said. "To stop them he would have to raise his hand against them. And we never oppose evil with evil."

"What do you call tar and feathering?"

The big farmer smiled. "Just deserts."

Heigstrom walked up to him and put a hand to his chest. "I won't stand for this. Off you go, Morg, and take these others with you."

A man behind Morganstern piped up with, "We won't be put off. He's an outsider. You shouldn't be protecting him."

"I am the law, Dwight. I protect everyone."

"Except liquor and corset salesmen," Fargo said.

Heigstrom glanced at him in annoyance. "You're not helping your cause."

"Stand aside, Pietor," Morganstern said, "or we will by God go through you."

"I'm warning you. I'll arrest anyone who tries to take the law into their own hands. This isn't those drummers all over again. This man is on official business. We must not do him physical harm."

"A little tar and feathers never hurt anybody," Morganstern said.

"The answer is still no."

"We're not asking, Pietor," declared a third of the crop-growing vigilantes.

"We want him and that's final," said yet another.

Heigstrom balled his fists. "I will fight you on this."

Morganstern balled his, which were twice as large, and held one up. "I can split a door with these. You've seen me with your own eyes."

"You threaten me now?"

Fargo had had enough. He picked up the Colt and slid it into his holster and then picked up the Henry and jacked the lever to feed a cartridge into the chamber.

That got their attention. Heigstrom and Morganstern stopped arguing and looked his way. Behind the huge farmer, faces tried to peer past.

Fargo leveled the Henry. "I'm leaving, and I'll shoot any of you idiots who tries to stop me."

"Now see here," Heigstrom said. "You're in my custody until I say otherwise."

"Like hell. I'm on official army business, as you just pointed out, and you jackasses are in my way."

"You won't kill me," Heigstrom blustered. "I'm an officer of the law."

"You're right," Fargo said. "I won't kill you. But I'll put a slug in your leg and in anyone else who doesn't move."

"You can't shoot all of us, mister," Morganstern growled.

"Care to bet?" Fargo said.

"I took an oath when I pinned this on," Heigstrom said, tapping his badge. "It's my duty to stop you and I by God will."

Fargo had hoped to convince them to back down. They were farmers, not gunmen. Now that his bluff had been called, he had a decision to make. Should he shoot or not? He made up his mind as Heigstrom came at him and grabbed for the Henry. Sidestepping, he drove the muzzle into the pit of the lawman's gut, doubling him over. A swift stroke of the butt, and he clubbed Heigstrom to the floor.

Morganstern let out a tremendous bellow, spread his arms wide, and charged.

Fargo shot him in the leg, in the fleshy part of the right thigh where it shouldn't do much harm. Most men would have crumpled on the spot but the huge farmer let out another bellow, gave a slight hop, and kept coming.

"Damn it," Fargo said, and shot him in the other thigh.

Morganstern pitched to his hands and knees. But he didn't stay there. Roaring like a stricken bull, he began to push to his feet.

Fargo clubbed him. Once, twice, a third time. At each blow Morganstern's head rocked, but not until the third did his eyes flutter and he collapsed in a heap.

Fargo raised the Henry to cover the others, thinking that might be the end of it.

He was wrong.

The rest poured through the doorway toward him.

35

Fargo was trying his damnedest not to take a life but they were making it hard. He slammed the Henry's barrel against the face of the first, swiveled, and used his boot on a knee of the second. Both men crashed down. An outflung hand clutched at his leg but he wrenched free and waded into the others.

The confines worked in his favor. Only one of them could come through the door at a time, and they had to step over those who were already down.

Wielding the Henry in a blur, Fargo clubbed two more. For a moment the doorway was clear. He jumped over a thrashing form and sprang out. A fist arced at his head but he ducked and retaliated by ramming the Henry's stock against a bearded chin.

"Stop him!" someone yelled.

Gripping the barrel in both hands, Fargo struck right and left. Faces burst with blood and fingers and wrists audibly cracked. Then the aisle before him was open and he raced to the front door.

People in the street had heard the shots. It was so unusual an occurrence that everyone had stopped what they were doing and turned toward the implement store.

"Look there!" a man shouted as Fargo broke into the light of day.

"It's the scout!" someone else hollered.

Fargo sprinted down the street. For once he was in luck in that the good folks of Titusville went around unarmed. No shots were sent his way.

A man in homespun moved to block him but Fargo pointed the Henry and the man thought better of it.

The Ovaro had its head high and its ears pricked. A quick getaway was nothing new, and no sooner was Fargo in the saddle than the stallion wheeled and broke into a gallop.

Fargo rode like blazes for the end of town. He was mildly startled when a rifle spanged but the shot missed. No others were fired.

Once the last of the buildings was behind him, Fargo rode hell-bent for leather to get as far away as he could before a posse came after him.

After a quarter of a mile or so he drew rein and looked back. Stick figures were moving about but no riders had appeared.

Puzzled, Fargo rode on. He had gone about half a mile when he came on one of several streams that accounted for why the valley was so green. The gently flowing water wasn't more than a few inches deep. Riding down into it, he followed its meandering course a short distance to some trees. Cottonwoods, mostly.

Dismounting, he stepped to a tree at the edge of the grass that stretched to Titusville, and climbed. He was playing a hunch. Isaiah Williams lived either in Titusville or on one of the surrounding farms. If the latter, it could be that Marshal Heigstrom would ride out to warn Williams that he was after him.

Roosting in a fork, he scanned the valley to the north and south of town. Here and there farmhouses and barns stood amid the cultivated fields. Most were painted red for some reason. It was as peaceful a scene as he could imagine, more fitting for a place like Ohio or Indiana than New Mexico Territory.

Fargo hated to think that this was how the entire territory would look one day. The tame life wasn't for him. For as long as he drew breath, he'd seek out the wild places where a man was free to roam as he pleased.

A rider had appeared, galloping out of Titusville to the north. It was too far for him to tell who it was. In a god-awful hurry, the rider passed several farms before he reined into a lane that brought him to a farmhouse shaded by oaks and maples.

Fargo debated. To go there in broad daylight invited discovery. It would be best to wait until dark.

Truth to tell, he could use a little rest. Descending, he sat with his back to the bole, folded his arms and rested his chin on his chest. In no time he'd drifted off.

A stomp of the Ovaro's hoof woke him. In reflex he put his hand on his Colt.

Across the stream and up it a short way, a coyote had come out of the brush to drink. It froze when it saw it wasn't alone, and as Fargo turned, it whirled and was gone.

Fargo rose and grinned at the Ovaro. "Scared of coyotes now?"

Forking leather, he headed for that farm.

Twilight was falling. Save for a few lingering streaks of red and orange on the western horizon, the blue sky had faded to gray and a few stars sparkled.

Fargo hoped he was right. He wanted to get this hunt over with. There were still Skeeter and Pratt to find but he was in no hurry where they were concerned. Not when they were the ones who'd raped the girl. Let Cuchillo Colorado have them. The bastards had it coming.

The windows of farmhouses glowed rosy with the light of newly lit lamps. Off in Titusville, more lit windows broke the darkling silhouettes of the buildings.

A welcome breeze had picked up. Fargo pushed his hat back on his head and ignored a grumble from his belly.

Suddenly several large animals rose out of the grass. But they were only cows that stood staring and chewing their cuds as he went by.

Night fell. At length he came to a stop two hundred yards out from the farmhouse the rider had visited. Circling wide, he warily approached the rear of the barn.

From the house came loud voices, as of an argument.

Fargo dismounted and let the reins dangle. He stalked around the side of the barn and was almost to the front when he caught movement close by.

Before he could think to flatten, a large dog appeared out of the gloom.

36

Fargo braced for a bark or a yip but all the dog did was stare. If it rushed him, he would try to club it with the Colt before it alerted the people in the farmhouse. He started to slowly draw so as not to incite it into attacking when it wagged its tail and walked up to him and sniffed.

Then it pressed its wet nose to his hand on the Colt and licked him.

"You're some guard dog," Fargo said quietly.

The dog's tail wagged harder and it uttered a friendly whine.

"The Apaches must love you," Fargo said, and went to go around.

The dog went with him, prancing happily at his side, wagging that tail a mile a minute.

"You are next to worthless," Fargo whispered, and the dog licked him again.

The loud voices had subsided in the farmhouse. He crept to the back door and peered in at an empty kitchen. A coffeepot sat on a potbellied stove and a loaf of bread and several slices were on a counter along with a carving knife.

Cautiously, Fargo tried the latch. To his surprise, the door wasn't bolted. It amazed him no end that anyone would leave a door unbarred in Apache country. Some folks were too trusting for their own good.

About to slip in, Fargo drew up short when the dog barred his way. For a few moments he thought it wouldn't let him, but no, it only wanted to lick him some more.

Plumb worthless, he almost said, and eased the dog aside with his leg. It whined again as he ducked in but not loud enough that the people inside would hear.

Closing the door, Fargo crossed to a hallway. Muted talk came from a doorway on the right. That would be the parlor, he reckoned. He was about to step out when footsteps pattered on stairs.

Someone was coming down from the second floor.

Pulling back, Fargo risked a peek.

A vision of loveliness swirled into view, a girl in her early twenties. She wore a plain white dress that clung to her in such a way as to show there was nothing plain about her. She had hair the color of straw and a lithe grace to every movement.

Fargo watched her go into the parlor. Careful not to let his spurs jingle, he sidled along the wall.

He figured that there would be Isaiah Williams and his wife, and the girl, and that would be all. He figured wrong.

A middle-aged couple in farm clothes sat on a settee and the girl was in a chair, and there were two others. A boy not much older than the girl was in another chair, and over by the front window stood none other than Marshal Heigstrom. And wonder of wonders, he was wearing a revolver.

"I think you are wasting your time, Pietor," the farmer on the settee said. "How would he know where we live?"

"He's like a fox, that one," Heigstrom said.

Fargo realized they were talking about him.

"Poor Mr. Morganstern," the woman said. "Are you sure he will be all right?"

"That's what Dr. Adams told me," Heigstrom said. "In a month he'll be up and around and as good as new."

"Mr. Morganstern was the only one this scout shot?" the girl in the chair asked.

"As I told you when I got here, yes," Heigstrom said.

"Then he's not the ogre you make him out to be," the girl remarked.

"Did you forget the part about him bashing heads and breaking bones?"

"You told us he had a rifle and a pistol. Yet the only one he shot was Mr. Morganstern," the girl said. "It seems to me that if all he did was hit people instead of shooting them, he was trying not to hurt people more than he had to."

Fargo liked this girl. He liked her a lot.

"That's ridiculous, Charity," the woman on the settee said.

"A man has a gun and doesn't use it, he must have a reason," Charity insisted.

"What do you know of guns and such?" the older woman snipped.

"Now, now, Patience," the man beside her said, and patted her leg. "Our daughter always has had a mind of her own."

"Don't encourage her," the woman said.

The girl in the chair twisted toward the young man about her age. "How about you, brother? What do you think of this scout?"

"Yes, Isaiah," said the man on the settee. "He's after you, after all."

Fargo smothered an oath of surprise. He'd taken it for granted the man on the settee was Isaiah Williams.

The young one cleared his throat. He had the same straw hair as his sister and the same green eyes but a thinner build. "I wish he hadn't come."

"Of course you do, dear," the mother said.

"I wish none of it ever happened," the boy went on. "I wish I hadn't let Skeeter and Pratt talk me into going with Mr. Ostman. I should have stayed here with you."

"You're young, son," the father said. "When I was your age, I sowed a few wild oats, too."

Fargo wondered how prospecting for gold qualified as wild oats.

"There you go again, Solomon," Patience Williams said. "Encouraging him like you encourage her."

"I did it for us, Ma," Isaiah said. "For the family."

"Oh, posh," Patience said. "You did it because milking cows and plowing fields bores you. You did it for the excitement, for the adventure. So tell me. Has it become exciting enough for you yet?"

"Patience, don't," Solomon said, but his wife didn't heed.

"That terrible business with the Apache girl, and now you have a scout after you and Apaches out for your blood. You've put all of us in danger by your reckless antics."

"Oh, Ma," Charity said.

"Don't you dare," Patience snapped. "I'll put up with your father defending him but your brother did wrong and you know it."

Over by the window Marshal Heigstrom said wearily, "Let's not start bickering again, shall we? What's done is done."

"You have no say in this," Patience said. "You're not part of our family."

"I'm here to protect you in case the scout shows up," Heigstrom said.

"It will be on your head if he does," Patience said. "He was one man against the entire town and you couldn't hold him."

"That's not fair," Heigstrom said. "I do the best I can."

"It's nowhere near good enough."

Solomon scowled at his wife. "Stop your carping, woman. He's doing us a favor by being here."

"Don't you woman me," Patience said.

Charity snorted. "Listen to us. One big happy family."

Ignoring her, Patience said, "I'd like to know what this scout's intentions are."

Fargo chose that moment to walk in, level his Colt, and smile. "Why don't you ask him?"

37

Heigstrom froze in the act of bending toward the window to peer out.

Solomon Williams showed no surprise whatsoever. His wife glared.

Isaiah Williams gave a slight jump in his chair and clutched the arms.

As for Charity, she had the most interesting reaction of all of them. She looked him up and down and smiled in a way that suggested she liked what she saw.

"Don't anyone do anything stupid," Fargo said. "I'm not here to hurt any of you."

"How did you get past Killer?" Patience Williams demanded.

"Killer?" Fargo said.

"Our dog."

"That's one fearsome animal you have there, lady," Fargo said.

"Is he still alive or did you do him in?"

"I let him lick me and he liked how I tasted and here I am."

Charity laughed.

"You're not funny," Patience said. "Nothing about this business is."

"I agree," Fargo said. "Two men have died who shouldn't have."

"Which men?" Isaiah asked.

"Samuels and Ostman. Didn't the marshal, here, tell you?"

"Oh God," Isaiah said. "They had no hand in what my friends did to that Apache girl."

"I know," Fargo said. "Now, suppose you tell me where I can find these pards of yours."

As if he were nervous or scared, Isaiah raised his voice and said, "Skeeter and Pratt? I'd rather not."

"I'll find them anyway, sooner or later."

Again the boy spoke much too loudly. "Skeeter and Pratt won't be as easy to take as me."

"We'll get to that taking in a minute," Fargo said, and faced Heigstrom. "But first things first. Use two fingers and set your six-gun on the floor and kick it over here."

"What if I take you into custody instead?" Heigstrom said. "You won't kill me. You're working for the army. They wouldn't stand for it."

"Who has to kill you?" Fargo said. "Remember Morgan-stern?"

"You're lucky you didn't cripple him."

"I'd have to saw a leg off to cripple that ox," Fargo said. "Now, shuck the hardware or you'll be limping around like him for a while."

Licking his lips, Heigstrom stared at the Colt, apparently debating whether he should or he shouldn't. Finally he obeyed, but his kick was so weak, the revolver slid only halfway. As if he were afraid Fargo would be mad at him, he said, "I'm not used to kicking things. Want me to kick it again?"

"Stay where you are," Fargo said.

"How about me?" Charity said. "Would you care to search me to see if I'm carrying a gun?"

"Charity!" Patience exclaimed.

"I was only joshing, Ma."

The girl winked at Fargo and he grinned. He liked her more by the minute. It took an effort to concentrate on why he was there. "I'm taking Isaiah to Fort Union. Not because I think he's guilty of anything. It's the one place in the terri-tory he'll be somewhat safe from Cuchillo Colorado."

"Hold on," Solomon said. "You're not taking my son any-where."

"If I don't get him out of here, Cuchillo Colorado will find him and do things to him that would curdle your blood," Fargo warned.

"How would that savage find us?" Patience asked.

"I did," Fargo said. He turned to the boy. "How is it you got involved, anyhow? You're a farmer, not an ore hound."

123

"My pa and Mr. Ostman were friends. He stopped by one day on his way to meet Samuels and go off prospecting, and I asked if I could go along. Ma didn't want me to but Pa said yes so I rode into town and told Skeeter and Pratt and they wanted to come along."

"Why them?" Fargo asked.

"They're my friends."

"They're vermin, is what they are," Patience interjected. "Look at all the trouble they've gotten you into."

"I never expected them to do anything like that," Isaiah said. He paled and bowed his head. "I can still hear the sounds in my head. . . ."

"And you did nothing," Fargo said.

"What could I do?" Isaiah said plaintively. "I didn't have a gun and both of them do. I begged them not to as they were dragging her into the tent but they told me to mind my own business."

"Some friends," Fargo said.

"I used to admire them," Isaiah said quietly. "How they lived as they pleased and never took guff off of anybody."

"You have a good life here," Patience said. "You had no call to go traipsing off with those no-accounts."

"I thought it would be fun to prospect for a while," Isaiah said. "Mr. Ostman offered to teach me. He was real nice."

"And now he's real dead," Fargo said. "As dead as you'll be if you don't let me help you."

"You're just saying that to scare me."

"I'm saying it because it's true. Cuchillo Colorado is on a vendetta and he won't stop this side of the grave."

Suddenly a hard object gouged the base of Fargo's spine and a voice snarled, "Speaking of graves, if you move that gun hand of yours, mister, they'll be putting you in one."

38

It was rare for someone to take Fargo so completely by surprise. He hadn't heard a sound, not so much as the scrape of a boot sole. Glancing over his shoulder, he saw why.

The man was in his stocking feet. Although calling him a man was a stretch. He looked younger than Isaiah. His cold gray eyes didn't fit with his freckles and pug nose. His clothes were the kind you could buy at any general store, and he wore a bowler. His Remington was cocked and his trigger finger set to squeeze. Reaching around, he relieved Fargo of the Colt.

"Let me guess," Fargo said. "Skeeter Bodine."

"Heard of me, have you?"

"I heard you were scum," Fargo said.

Skeeter's smirk widened and his hand flicked and the Remington caught Fargo across the cheek. "Insult me again. I dare you."

Fargo's head was rocked but he didn't lose any teeth and he wasn't bleeding. He almost threw caution aside and sprang, but another had appeared behind Skeeter, holding a Smith & Wesson in one hand and a pair of boots in the other.

"Say howdy to Billy Pratt," Skeeter taunted. "He doesn't say much but he will kill you as quick as anything."

"Howdy, mister," Pratt said.

Patience rose from the settee. "How dare you come into our house waving guns."

"Who's waving?" Skeeter said. "And sit back down, you old bag."

"Skeeter," Isaiah said.

Patience took a step toward Skeeter but Solomon grabbed

125

her wrist and pulled her down onto the settee. She tried to wrench free but couldn't.

"Get ahold of yourself, wife," he said.

Skeeter stepped back and slid Fargo's Colt under his belt. Holding his hand out to Pratt, he said, "Give me my boots and cover him while I put them on."

Pratt waggled his Smith & Wesson. "Why don't you have a seat on the floor there, mister? It will keep you from getting ideas."

His cheek throbbing, Fargo sat cross-legged, his right hand resting on his pant leg where it met his boot. He could feel the slight bulge of his ankle sheath and the Arkansas toothpick.

Heigstrom, who hadn't uttered a word in a while, cleared his throat and said, "Where the devil did you boys come from? I looked all over town for you earlier and couldn't find you."

Pratt had sunk to the floor and was tugging on his left boot. "Someone got word to us about this one," he said, with a nod at Fargo. "So we lit out and Isaiah hid us in his barn."

"He did what?" Patience said.

"They're my friends," Isaiah said. "What else could I do?"

"They are not," Patience said. "The only ones they care about are themselves."

"I am growing tired of you, lady," Skeeter said.

"You'd best be careful how you talk about us."

"She's my mother," Isaiah said.

"She's a damn nag," Skeeter said. He got the boot on and reached for the other. "But enough about her. We have to decide what to do about the scout, here."

"How do you mean?" Isaiah asked.

"How do you think?" Skeeter rejoined. "We can't let him drag us back to Fort Union. We have to make sure he leaves us be and there's only one way to do that."

Charity put a hand to her throat. "You wouldn't?"

"Of course they would," Patience said archly. "They force themselves on women, don't they?"

Pausing with his boot half on, Skeeter grew red in the face. "She was an Apache, for God's sake. It's not as if she was white."

"Her skin doesn't matter. She was a young woman and you had no right."

Fargo's estimation of Patience rose a notch. He kept hoping Pratt would let the muzzle of the Smith & Wesson dip but he held it rock-steady.

"She tried to steal our horses," Skeeter said, tugging. "And she killed my dog. The red bitch had it coming."

"You're despicable," Patience said.

"I am so tired of you I could scream," Skeeter said. He got the second boot on, and stood. He stamped them a few times, then took the Remington from Pratt and pointed it at Fargo. "Any last words?"

"No!" Charity cried.

"Skeeter, don't," Isaiah said.

"I will arrest you if you do," Heigstrom said. "It will be cold-blooded murder and you will be hung."

Skeeter gave all three a look of pure scorn. "There isn't one of you who sees it, is there?"

"Sees what?" Patience said.

"I let him take me, I'll end my days in prison. I read that newspaper. The government is out to make an example of me. And for what? Poking a damned Apache." Skeeter shook his head. "No, sir. That's not going to happen. I figure to light a shuck for Denver or maybe Oregon country where they'll never find me."

"Tuck your tail and run," Patience said. "I'd expect no less from a yellow-dog cur."

"Wife," Solomon said.

"I won't kowtow to this infant," Patience said. "He's despicable and deserves what is coming to him."

"So do you, lady," Skeeter said, and pointing his revolver, he shot her in the face.

39

For all of ten seconds everyone was riveted in shock. Then Solomon cried in anguish, "Wife!" and lunged to catch her body as it began to topple from the settee.

Charity screamed.

Isaiah let out with a "Noooo!" and came out of his chair and darted to the settee.

Marshal Heigstrom's mouth fell open and his eyes grew wide with horror.

Skeeter Bodine grinned.

Pratt, who was slightly behind him, threw back his head and laughed.

No one paid any attention to Fargo. No one saw him slip his hand into his boot and palm the Arkansas toothpick. No one was aware he was pushing to his feet until he was up, and then two swift bounds brought him to Skeeter.

The youthful killer was still grinning at what he'd done. His grin twisted into a snarl and he went to point his revolver at Fargo.

Fargo was quicker. He slashed the toothpick across Bodine's wrist, cutting as hard and as deep as he could.

Scarlet sprayed, and Skeeter howled and jerked back, his revolver thudding to the floor. He fell against Pratt. Both stumbled, and Skeeter tripped and went to his knees. He clutched at Fargo's Colt with his other hand but it slipped from his grasp and it, too, thunked to the floorboards.

Fargo threw himself to the right as Pratt snapped a shot that missed. Only a few feet away lay Heigstrom's six-shooter. He scrambled and snatched it up and rolled onto his back to shoot but Skeeter and Pratt were no longer there. Quickly, he slid the toothpick into his ankle sheath, pushed up, and darted to his Colt. With pistols in both hands, he poked his head into the hallway.

A shot boomed and Fargo pulled back. His glimpse had shown him Pratt and Skeeter frantically backpedaling and almost to the front door, Pratt with one arm around Skeeter to keep him from collapsing, Skeeter holding his severed wrist to his chest. Skeeter's arm and shirt were crimson and his features were contorted in agony.

"Hold on, there," Heigstrom found his voice. "Give me my gun."

Fargo poked out again and went to fire both revolvers but there was no one to shoot. The front door was wide open and a trail of red splotches led outside. He cast the marshal's revolver in Heigstrom's direction and ran after the twin causes of all the killing and misery.

At full speed he burst out onto the porch and flung himself flat. A six-shooter barked and wood splintered a rail.

Pratt and Skeeter were running for the barn, Skeeter swaying as if he were drunk. The loss of blood was getting to him.

Fargo crawled toward the steps to get a clear shot. Pratt fired again, and he was good. The slug nearly clipped Fargo's shoulder.

Just then Heigstrom blundered onto the porch. He stopped and looked about in confusion, saying, "What's going on? Where are they?"

Pratt's revolver spat smoke and noise.

Fargo heard the fleshy thwack of lead striking home. He heard a loud gasp and looked over his shoulder.

Heigstrom was staggering, a hand splayed to his chest. He fell against the house and stared down at himself in astonishment. "They shot me," he said in disbelief. "They honest to God shot me."

"Get down," Fargo said.

Heigstrom looked at him. "This is all your fault. If you hadn't come to town, none of this would have happened. Patience would still be alive and I wouldn't be shot."

Fargo had never met a more useless lawman in his life. He twisted around to go to him and pull him down before Pratt fired again.

"It doesn't hurt much," Heigstrom said. "I think he missed my heart and my lungs."

Over at the barn, Pratt's revolver cracked.

With the light from the hallway spilling over him, Heigstrom might as well have been wearing a bull's-eye. The slug caught him in the throat and slammed his head into the wall. His hat fell off and he uttered an inarticulate cry and broke into convulsions.

Fargo snapped a shot at the barn but Pratt and Skeeter were already inside.

Heigstrom slid down and came to rest, his arms limp at his sides, his mouth opening and closing but no sounds coming out.

"Damn it," Fargo said. He went to him and crouched. There was nothing he could do. The slug had torn clean through, leaving a hole big enough to stick two fingers in.

Blood was pumping by the pint.

Heigstrom somehow managed to speak. He got out, "All . . . your . . . fault." Red rivulets flowed from his nose and the corners of his mouth. He tried to say more, and died.

Hooves drummed. Pratt and Skeeter exploded from the barn at a gallop, Skeeter clinging to his saddle for dear life.

Fargo ran to the rail and fired but knew he missed. He thumbed the hammer to fire again and this time aimed at the center of a dark mass. His finger was tightening when a hand fell on his arm, jostling him. His hand jerked and the shot went wide.

The next moment the fleeing pair were swallowed by the darkness.

Skeeter and Pratt had gotten away.

40

The hand was still on Fargo's arm. He angrily went to swat it away, but didn't.

It was Charity, her eyes brimming with tears, her mouth quivering. "Please," she said. "Help us. My father. My brother."

"What about them?"

Instead of answering, Charity tugged on his arm and again said, "Please. Come quickly."

Reluctantly, Fargo let her pull him inside. He'd rather run to the Ovaro and light out after Skeeter and Pratt, even though the odds of finding them before daylight were slim. "What is it?"

"I don't know what to do," Charity said, and it was obvious she was barely holding herself together. "My mother . . ." She didn't finish.

Patience Williams lay on the floor of the parlor. Her hands had been placed on her bosom and she looked as if she were at rest except for the hole where her left eye had been.

Beside her, slumped in shock, was Solomon. His eyes were half glazed and he didn't seem to be breathing.

On the other side of her, Isaiah blubbered, tears and snot trickling down his face. He kept mewing, "Ma! Ma! Ma!"

Fargo realized why the boy hadn't done anything when his friends raped Corn Flower. Isaiah Williams was a spineless jellyfish.

"What do I do?" Charity appealed to him. "They won't either of them say anything. Watch." She took a breath. "Pa? Isaiah? We have to get hold of ourselves."

The father went on blankly staring at his dead wife and the son went on wailing.

Charity smothered a sob of her own. "How do I bring them out of it?"

"Like this." Fargo walked over to Solomon and smacked him across the face.

The blow rocked the farmer against the settee. Solomon blinked and shook his head and looked about him in confusion, saying, "What?"

Turning, Fargo bent and raised his arm to do the same to the son.

"Don't you dare!" Isaiah cried, and skittered out of reach.

Fargo's disgust knew no bounds. "Stop your damn bawling," he growled.

"My ma is dead," Isaiah exclaimed. "What else do you expect me to do?"

Charity was crying, too, but she wasn't putting on the display her brother was. "Please, Isaiah," she said, hunkering beside him and placing her arm on his shoulder. "This isn't helping."

"Leave me be," Isaiah said, shrugging her off. With a sob, he moved to his mother and pressed his face to her shoulder.

Solomon was wiping his eyes with a sleeve. "Your sister is right, boy. This is unbecoming. Act like a man for once."

"For once?" Fargo said.

Solomon coughed and his eyes watered but he didn't lose control. "He's always been like this. Any little thing would set him off. I've tried to get him to see that a man doesn't bawl his brains out when his cat dies or he breaks a finger when a bale of hay falls on it." The father took a deep breath. "Patience used to say he was born with a sensitive nature. She always coddled him. But not me. It's why I thought it would be a good idea for him to go prospecting. To get out and see what the real world is like."

Isaiah uttered a loud moan.

Fargo turned away. "I'll help with the bodies," he offered.

"Bodies?"

"Heigstrom is on the porch."

"Dear Lord. Not him too?" Solomon pushed to his feet and walked unsteadily out.

Fargo was going to follow but Charity clasped his hand.

"How long can you stay?"

"I aim to head out after those bastards at first light," Fargo informed her.

"Good. I was hoping you'd say that. I'm worried Skeeter and Pratt might come back."

Fargo didn't see why they would with him there, and said so.

"You don't know those two like I do. I never have liked them. Never have trusted them. They've always been after me to . . . you know." Charity's face flared with anger. "Whenever Ma and Pa weren't around, they'd make lewd remarks. Especially that Skeeter Bodine. Now and then he'd even put his hands on me. Once I slapped him and do you know what he did? He laughed. What my brother saw in them, I'll never know."

Insight flooded Fargo. Bodine hadn't befriended Isaiah Williams because he liked him. Bodine did it so he could get up Charity's dress. Which put the rape in a whole new light. It wasn't the random act of an Indian-hater. Skeeter Bodine lived for one thing and one thing only. He'd raped Corn Flower because he *liked* it.

"After we take care of Ma, I'll make coffee, if you'd like."

"I could use some," Fargo said. "But I can do it myself."

"No. I need to keep busy. And having someone to talk to will help." Charity looked at Isaiah, who was still weeping. "My poor brother," she said, to herself more than Fargo. "What are we to do with you?"

Fargo was thinking about Bodine and the other one. "Tell me," he said. "Do you have any notion of where I might find those two?"

"They were renting a room in town but I doubt they'd go there. I don't know where they're from originally. They'd pass through Titusville now and then and always made it a point to look Isaiah up. He met them a few years ago when we were in buying supplies and they hit it off."

Fargo imagined that Skeeter Bodine's first sight of her had a lot to do with it.

"One thing," Charity said, and gnawed her bottom lip. "I never put much credence in it but I guess I should have. Skeeter used to brag on himself to impress me. One time he showed up a bit tipsy and when we were alone he told me that he'd killed a man."

"Doesn't surprise me a bit," Fargo said.

"The thing you should know," Charity said, "is that he told me he'd shot the man in the back. And he laughed about it." She squeezed his fingers. "You'd better watch yours or he's liable to do the same to you."

Solomon Williams was standing on the porch staring down at Marshal Heigstrom with a look of utter defeat and sorrow. He barely reacted when Fargo nudged him.

"Where do you want to put the body?"

"Eh?"

"The body," Fargo said. "Are you going to leave it lying there?" He didn't care one way or the other. Heigstrom had been a fool. A well-meaning fool, but he'd had no business wearing a badge.

"Oh," Solomon said numbly. "I suppose the barn would be best. We don't want it in the house. It would only disturb Isaiah and Charity."

"I'll give you a hand," Fargo said. He slid his under Heigstrom's shoulders and got a good grip. "Take the other end."

Nodding, Solomon took hold of both legs.

Together, they lifted and moved down the steps.

Fargo stayed alert. Charity could be right about Skeeter and Pratt circling back. Although, as hurt as Bodine was, that didn't seem likely.

Solomon stared forlornly at the farmhouse. "Patience and me were married twenty-eight years this past June."

Fargo grunted.

"I loved her. Loved her dearly."

Fargo wondered why the man was telling him this. He chalked it up to grief.

"Some folks said she was crotchety. But she spoke her mind, that gal, and didn't care who she spoke it to."

Fargo grunted again.

"I admired that in her. Her spunk. You saw how she stood up to that Bodine."

And got herself shot, Fargo reflected.

"I don't know what I'll do without her. She was my whole life."

"You still have Charity and Isaiah."

"Isaiah," Solomon said bitterly. "Patience shouldn't have coddled him like she did. But I can't hold it against her. It was her nature to protect those she cared for."

Fargo was walking backward and glanced over his shoulder at the barn. The door, he saw, had been left half-open.

"Do you have any children?" the farmer unexpectedly asked.

"I hope not but I might."

"How can you not know? Don't tell me you're one of those who is fond of fallen doves and other ladies of loose repute, as Patience used to call them?"

"More than fond," Fargo admitted.

"I only ever knew Patience," Solomon said. "She was all I ever wanted."

They were almost to the barn. Fargo shifted his hands to get a better grip.

"Say, what's that?" Solomon said, looking past him. "Be careful or you'll trip."

Fargo stopped and looked behind him. Almost at his feet lay a sprawled form. "It's your dog."

"What?" Solomon suddenly let go of the marshal's legs and they thumped to the ground. Rushing up, he knelt. "Killer? My God. His throat has been slit."

Fargo set the marshal down.

"Damn Bodine and that Pratt, anyhow," Solomon said. "They had no cause to do this. Killer knew them from all the times they've been here. Hell, Bodine used to like to pet him and have him fetch a stick."

"He did?" Fargo said, and a silent warning jangled.

"I'm not a violent man but if I could get my hands on those two. . . ." Solomon stopped and muttered something under his breath.

Fargo cocked his head. He'd heard the slightest of sounds and now he spied movement. Instinct galvanized him into throwing himself at Williams and shoving him flat even as the night exploded with rifle fire.

"What in the world?" Solomon bleated.

Streaking his Colt from its holster, Fargo fired at the muzzle flashes. With his other hand he gripped Solomon and pushed him at the barn door. "Get inside!"

Crabbing on his hands and knees, the farmer made it in.

Fargo followed, keeping low. Once behind the door, he rose.

"They came back," Solomon fumed. "They murdered my wife and the marshal and they have the gall to come back and try to finish us off."

"I don't think it's them," Fargo said. He was probing the night but it was deathly still.

"Then who?"

"Cuchillo Colorado."

"The Apache? Why would he be here?"

"Cuchillo Colorado is after Bodine and Pratt and Isaiah, remember?" Fargo said while continuing to seek some sign of the warriors.

"Yes, but what I meant was, how could he have found where we live?" Solomon said, and stiffened. "My son! They'll try to hurt Isaiah." And with that, he raced into the open yelling at the top of his lungs, "Isaiah! Isaiah! The Apaches are here!"

"Don't!" Fargo yelled. Swearing, he ran after him. "Get down, damn you!"

A rifle boomed and it was as if Solomon had slammed into a wall. He clutched at his chest, screamed, "Isaiah!" and crumpled.

Fargo caught him. Life had already faded and the body was limp. He flattened, expecting shots to be directed at him.

Instead, inside the farmhouse, Charity Williams screamed in terror.

42

Fargo levered erect and dashed for the house. He zigzagged to make himself harder to hit and was puzzled by why he wasn't shot at.

On reaching the porch he took the steps in a bound. Flinging the door wide, he charged down the hall to the parlor. He was being reckless but it couldn't be helped. If the Apaches got their hands on Isaiah, well, so be it. But Charity was another matter.

He reached the parlor and did more swearing.

Patience Williams lay where he had last seen her. A chair had been overturned and there were fresh drops of blood on the floor leading to the hall and down it toward the kitchen.

Fargo flew. The drops continued through the kitchen to the back door. He hurtled out and turned right and left, but no one, nothing.

Fury boiled in his veins. He tilted his head and listened intently but once again, nothing.

First Skeeter Bodine and Pratt had gotten away, and now this.

Going after the Apaches in the dark would be pointless. The smart thing to do was wait until daylight. But the mere thought of waiting that long, of an innocent girl like Charity in the clutches of Cuchillo Colorado and Culebra Negro, made him want to mount up and search anyway.

Suddenly Fargo had a chilling thought. The Ovaro! He'd tied the stallion out in back of the barn. What if the Apaches had found it?

Whirling, Fargo sprinted like a madman around the house and past Solomon's body. He let out a sigh of relief when he saw the stallion was where he'd left it, its ears pricked from all the commotion. Running over, he untied it and vaulted onto the saddle.

He should ride to the house or maybe go into the barn and stay there until dawn broke, but instead he rode in a wide circle, listening.

As he neared the west side of the house he was sure he heard faint hoofbeats. Since Skeeter and Pratt had gone south, it must be the Apaches. Only they hadn't had horses the last time he saw them. Given that they were masters at stealing them, that meant nothing.

Hoping he wasn't making a mistake, Fargo headed west. He held to a trot and stopped every now and then. Each time he did, far to the west hooves drummed. If it was the Apaches, they were being uncommonly careless. Or it could be that now that they had Isaiah and the girl, they were anxious to get as far away as they could before word spread and the whole countryside was aroused.

Fargo pressed on. An hour passed, and then two.

It was obvious the Apaches were making for the end of the valley and the open country beyond. Once there, they could lose themselves in the vastness of terrain they knew so well.

Fatigue nipped at Fargo but he shrugged it off. He'd rest when this was over, not before.

A pink fringe of sky, herald to the new day, found him amid dry hills dotted by boulders and stone monoliths.

He kept scouring the ground, and as a golden arch was dimming the stars, he found tracks. When he saw how many, he drew rein to study them.

He counted six different horses. None were shod. Instead of four warriors to deal with, he now had six. Where the other two came from, he had no idea.

Fargo drew his Colt and inserted a sixth cartridge. Normally, like a lot of frontiersmen and gun hands, he kept only five in the cylinder so the hammer rested on an empty chamber, a precaution for safety's sake. But now he reckoned he'd need that extra cartridge before too long.

The Apaches had made no attempt to hide their trail. Yet another puzzlement. Or it could be that with the valley behind them, they figured they were safe.

Overconfidence wasn't an exclusive trait of the white man.

Fargo was thankful they hadn't stopped yet. Charity would be safe until they did. Even then, when it came to their enemies, Apaches liked to toy with them like cats toyed with mice. It might be a while before they got around to doing to her what had been done to Corn Flower.

Or so he hoped.

The middle of the morning came and went and still the Apaches pressed on.

Fargo was beginning to think they would ride the whole day through. At least they'd slowed to a walk, which spared the Ovaro.

The sun was a yellow furnace in the vault of sky when the stallion raised its head and stared to the northwest.

Fargo looked but didn't see anything except higher hills. Slowing, he cautiously advanced and soon discovered that the Apaches had reined toward them.

He had a hunch he was near the end of the chase. From here on out he couldn't afford a mistake.

The tracks wound deeper in.

The Apaches had been riding in single file and never once did a warrior break off and climb to the top of a hill to check their back trail. More of that overconfidence.

He was surprised when he smelled smoke. Drawing rein, he dismounted, yanked the Henry from the saddle scabbard, and was about to stalk forward when he remembered to remove his spurs. The slightest jingle could give him away.

As silently as possible, Fargo went up the slope of the nearest hill. About halfway he crouched and slowly worked around until he could see the lay of the land ahead.

Not quite fifty yards from the hill was an oval basin. The sides were steep and littered with small stones except for a twenty-foot section that had buckled, creating a dirt ramp to the bottom.

Fargo wondered why the Apaches had picked there to stop. A glimmer of water amid some boulders gave him the answer. It was a tank, one of the many secret watering places known only to the Apaches.

Six weary horses stood with their heads hanging. As for the Apaches, they had kindled a small fire and four of the six had squatted around it and were talking and at ease.

Cuchillo Colorado was there, and Culebra Negro, too.

That fire bothered Fargo. The only reason to make one in the heat of the day was to cook but he saw no evidence of dead game.

He didn't see the captives and that bothered him more. Then a fifth Apache appeared, his rifle leveled at the captives he was leading from the tank amid the boulders.

Only there weren't two captives, as Fargo expected. There were four.

Charity came first, her wrists bound behind her back, her head down and her hair over her face. After her stumbled Isaiah. It was plain he was scared clean through.

The other two captives were a surprise, although in hindsight, Fargo reckoned they shouldn't be. The Apaches must have arrived at the farm earlier than he'd thought and been watching when Skeeter Bodine and Pratt made their break.

Now both were in the hands of the vengeful warrior whose daughter they had violated.

Pratt glared defiantly at his captors and snarled something at the warrior holding the rifle.

Skeeter moved as if drunk. The whole front of his shirt was red with the blood he'd lost, and he was as pale as paper.

Cuchillo Colorado rose and smiled. Walking up to Charity, he cupped her chin. Wisely, she didn't fight him. He made a remark that caused the other Apaches to laugh. Then he stepped to Isaiah and reached for his chin but Isaiah jerked back in fear.

Glowering, Cuchillo Colorado cuffed him so hard, Isaiah's legs almost buckled.

Pratt met glare with glare.

Skeeter Bodine didn't even raise his head when Cuchillo Colorado moved to him. The Apache put his hand on the hilt of his knife but didn't draw it. Whatever he said brought grim countenances to the rest of the warriors.

Fargo wouldn't want to be in Bodine's boots. Apaches were masters at torturing an enemy. They could draw it out for hours. For days, in some instances. He imagined that by the time Cuchillo Colorado was done, Skeeter Bodine would be worse than Samuels had been.

Fargo would like to wait until nightfall and then slip in

but there was no telling how long the Apaches would hold off on Charity. Culebra Negro, in fact, was looking at her as if she were a prime slice of beef and he was half starved.

The captives were made to sit. Isaiah immediately threw himself flat and whimpered and cried.

Keeping low, Fargo scrambled back until he was out of sight, and stood. He aimed to sneak to the basin and drop as many as he could with the Henry. If he downed three or four of them before they knew what hit them, he stood a chance.

He was almost to the Ovaro when he realized the stallion was staring up the slope he'd just descended. Staring at something or someone above him.

Fargo went to turn just as a battering ram slammed between his shoulder blades.

43

The impact sent Fargo tumbling hat over boots. His hat went flying and so did the Henry. With a bone-jarring jolt he came to rest on his back. For a few seconds the sky spun crazily.

Instinctively, Fargo clutched for his Colt only to have his hand swatted aside. He stabbed for it again but his holster was empty. He heard a click just as his head cleared and he found himself staring up into the muzzle of his own cocked six-shooter.

The Apache holding it had a face as hard as flint.

Fargo knew that one twitch and he'd be dead.

The warrior didn't appear to know the white tongue. He barked in his own, telling Fargo to stand, slowly, as he backed off, keeping the Colt trained on Fargo's face. In his other hand he held a rifle.

Fargo stood. The pain from his fall was fading.

The Apache motioned for him to head for the basin, then snagged the stallion's reins. He also scooped up the Henry, holding it and his own rifle by their barrels, and the reins, all in one hand.

Fargo felt like the world's biggest dunce. The warrior must have been posted as a lookout on the hill he'd climbed. He'd been so intent on what was going on in the basin that he hadn't even thought to look for sign of anyone higher up. Not that he would have seen him if the Apache didn't want him to.

The other warriors came to their feet the moment he appeared. Cuchillo Colorado smiled. Culebra Negro looked as if he'd just been given a present he'd always wanted. The others spread out, ready.

As for the captives, Charity beamed and cried out, "Fargo!"

Isaiah looked up, showed no expression, and bowed his head again.

Skeeter Bodine was too weak to do more than glance over. Pratt glared.

The Ovaro caught the smell of the water in the tank and nickered and tried to pull away but the warrior held on to the reins.

His smile widening, Cuchillo Colorado stepped around the fire. "We meet again, white-eye."

"Lucky me," Fargo said.

"I have the last of them," Cuchillo Colorado gloated, with a sweep of his arm at his prisoners.

"Plus one," Fargo said.

"She is sister to the weak one," Cuchillo Colorado said, as if that explained why he'd taken her.

"She had no part in what they did to Corn Flower," Fargo said. "Let her go."

"You know I will not."

"What do you aim to do with her?"

"What do you think?"

"Then you are no better than the men who raped your daughter," Fargo said with as much scorn as he could muster.

Cuchillo Colorado lost his smile.

"Let me kill this one," Culebra Negro requested.

"*To-dah*. Not yet," Cuchillo Colorado said. "He Who Walks Many Trails will die the same as the rest after the rest." His smile returned. "My gift to you, scout."

"You call killing me a gift?" Fargo said.

"You helped me find them," Cuchillo Colorado said, and gestured at Isaiah and Skeeter and Pratt. "And those first two."

"Samuels and Ostman didn't have a hand in the rape and you damn well know it." Fargo knew he was wasting his breath. They'd been through all this.

A gleam of pure hate came into Cuchillo Colorado's dark eyes and he pointed at Skeeter and then at Pratt. "They did."

"And him?" Fargo said, bobbing his chin at Isaiah. "What excuse do you have for killing him other than you just like to kill whites?"

Those dark eyes glittered brighter. "I like. I like killing white-eyes more than anything."

144

Isaiah, who had raised his head to listen, covered his face with his hands and wailed, "Oh God!"

To a man, the Apaches regarded him with contempt. To them, the true test of a warrior was how well he held up under hardship. Isaiah Williams was the opposite of their ideal. He was a sniveling infant, and merited their utmost contempt.

Cuchillo Colorado turned to two of his companions and had them bind Fargo's wrists and put him with the other captives.

Fargo didn't resist. To do so would be stupid. He needed to bide his time and hope that fortune favored him with a way to turn the tables. Otherwise, his bleached bones would gleam white in the hot sun for a long time.

"You came after us," Charity said as he sank beside her.

"I came after you," Fargo corrected her.

"What about me?" Isaiah sniffled. "You're not here to rescue me, too?"

Instead of answering, Fargo said, "You could have spared yourself all this if you'd stood up to your friends when they got their hands on Corn Flower."

"What could I do? I'm no fighter."

"He sure as hell ain't," Pratt threw in.

"Forget all that," Charity said. "The important thing is what are we going to do *now*? How can we get out of this fix?"

"I wish it were a dream," Isaiah said. "Nothing but a bad dream, and I'll wake up in bed and everything will be fine."

"Jackass," Pratt said.

"Hold on a minute," Charity said, gazing at the hills to the east. "Where's my pa?" she asked Fargo. "Didn't he come with you?"

Fargo had forgotten that the daughter and the son had no idea their father was dead. He shook his head.

"Why not? Where is he?" Charity asked. "He wouldn't stay behind with us in peril."

"No," Isaiah said, "he wouldn't."

"He didn't make it," Fargo said.

"Didn't . . . ?" Charity said, and gasped. She paled and tears welled and she said softly, "Not Pa, too? Not both of them."

"Our pa is dead?" Isaiah said. "He's not going to save us?"

"I'm all you have," Fargo told him.

"And look at how worthless you've proven to be," Isaiah said bitterly.

Fargo was about to tell him to go to hell but just then Cuchillo Colorado and Culebra Negro approached.

"We are ready to start," the former said, and made a show of looking thoughtfully at each of them. "Who dies first?"

"Pick him," Culebra Negro said, indicating Fargo.

Cuchillo Colorado grinned and pointed at the one he'd chosen.

44

Skeeter Bodine died a horrible death.

The Apaches seized him by his arms and legs—a warrior on each limb—and carried him over close to the fire and pinned him on his back on the ground. He struggled weakly and pleaded for his life.

Then Cuchillo Colorado drew his knife and moved between Bodine's legs.

"Don't look," Fargo said to Charity, and she gulped and averted her face.

Isaiah uttered a shriek at the first stab of the knife, and collapsed, blubbering.

Pratt swore viciously.

Fargo counted ten thrusts of the red blade before Cuchillo Colorado was satisfied. The whole time, Bodine screamed and thrashed.

That was just the start.

Cuchillo Colorado whittled on him for pretty near half an hour. The parts he cut off, he tossed into a pile. When he finally sat back, his fingers and forearms were splashed scarlet and Skeeter Bodine was gibbering as if he'd lost his mind.

Rising, Cuchillo Colorado used his knife to roll two red coals from the fire onto a flat rock. He carefully carried the rock over to Bodine and knelt. At a word from him, Culebra Negro knelt, too, and gripped Bodine's head so he couldn't move it.

"What are you doing?" Skeeter screeched.

Fargo had some notion of what to expect but it still sickened him.

Cuchillo Colorado held the flat rock over Bodine's right eye. Using the tip of his knife, he rolled a coal onto it.

Bodine's shriek seemed to shake the hills.

Cuchillo Colorado did the same to the other eye and the Apaches watched as both sizzled.

Usually burning someone's eyes out wasn't enough to kill them. The Apaches were considerably surprised when, after a minute or two of screams and wails, Skeeter Bodine stiffened and arched his back and went limp.

The Apaches waited, and when their victim showed no signs of life, Culebra Negro moved Bodine's head back and forth and slapped his cheek several times. *"Tats-an,"* he said.

The Apache word for dead.

Charity and Isaiah were both crying.

Pratt was tight-lipped.

Fargo felt nothing. While he didn't think that anyone deserved so grisly an end, Bodine had brought it on himself. Raping a woman was vile. If he'd been white, Bodine would have wound up at the end of a rope. Apaches weren't as merciful.

Cuchillo Colorado came over, still holding his bloodstained knife. "I avenge Corn Flower. In a while we do one more of you."

"I didn't do anything!" Isaiah wailed.

"That is why," Cuchillo Colorado said, and walked away.

While the torture was going on, Fargo had bent his legs so that his boots were under his hands. Moving only when he was sure none of the Apaches were looking his way, he'd slid his pant leg up and eased his fingers into his boot. Just as Cuchillo Colorado was rolling the first red-hot coal off the rock, he'd slipped the Arkansas toothpick from its ankle sheath. Now, reversing his grip, he held it on the inside of his forearms, out of sight.

The Apaches were in good spirits. They squatted around the fire and talked, and now and again one would point at what was left of Skeeter Bodine and say something that made the others smile.

Fargo got busy cutting the rope. His toothpick was razor sharp; he made it a point to hone it often. The strands parted but not fast enough to suit him. He pressed harder.

Charity was the only one of the captives who saw what he

was doing. When she did, she shifted so that she helped block the view of the warriors in case any looked over.

Fargo smiled his appreciation and went on slicing.

Isaiah wouldn't stop mewing. He was a wreck. Twice he glanced at Bodine and uttered wails that the Apaches found hilarious.

All Pratt did was glare. He was hard, that one. Fargo had a hunch the Apaches wouldn't have the satisfaction of hearing him beg.

It seemed to take forever for the toothpick to do its work. But at last the rope parted and Fargo's hands were free. "I'll do you next," he whispered to Charity, and turned slightly so he could.

The Apaches were apparently in no hurry. They sent one of their number to the top of the nearby hill and when he came back he reported that he'd seen no sign of anyone on their back trail.

By then Fargo had cut Charity free. He didn't free Isaiah. The fool was bound to give it away and bring the warriors down on them.

Fargo glanced at Pratt, who was the farthest away. "Slide toward me real slow and I'll do you, too," he whispered.

"I don't want no help from you. You only want to turn me over to the army."

"We have a bigger worry," Fargo whispered, nodding at the Apaches.

"I won't let you take me."

"Use your damn head."

"I always do. I was always the smart one. Skeeter was just reckless. He'd get into trouble and I'd have to get him out."

"Let me cut you free."

"No need. I already am." Pratt moved his arms just enough to show that he indeed was.

"How?" Fargo wanted to know.

"You're not the only hombre who carries a hideout in his boot. I have a pocket bowie."

Fargo had seen them. Small versions of the larger, more famous kind. Most had blades about five inches long and were only half as wide.

"We do this right," Pratt whispered, "we can kill two of

these stinking savages before they know we're loose. That will only leave four."

"Only?" Fargo said.

"Count me in," Charity whispered. "I want to help."

"What can you do?" Pratt said. "Scratch their eyes out?"

"I'll do what I can."

"No," Fargo told her. "When we make our move, I want you to grab your brother and get the hell out of here. With any luck, we'll keep them busy long enough for you to get away."

"That wouldn't be right."

"Would you rather be dead?"

"You'd be smart to leave your brother and go by yourself," Pratt whispered. "He's a worthless gob of spit."

"Don't talk about him like that," Charity bristled. "And what do you know, anyhow?"

"I know your brother won't be of any use when we're fighting for our lives."

"He's always been weak-willed," Charity said. "It's just how he is. You can't hold it against him."

"Cuchillo Colorado does," Fargo said.

As if he had heard them, Cuchillo Colorado chose that moment to look over at them.

"Here it comes," Pratt said. "He's making up his mind which of us to whittle on next."

Fargo had thought Isaiah wasn't listening but he mewed, "It'll be me. I know it will. He hates me because I didn't stop you and Skeeter from hurting that poor girl."

"Why you people keep making a fuss over a damned Apache, I'll never know," Pratt said angrily, raising his voice. "She deserved it."

"No woman ever deserves *that*," Charity said.

Their argument might have gone on but just then Cuchillo Colorado rose and came toward them.

"Uh-oh," Charity said.

45

Fargo firmed his hold on the toothpick. He was counting on the element of surprise but that wouldn't buy them more than a few seconds. He wished Cuchillo Colorado had a gun but the Apache's rifle was over by the fire.

Unexpectedly, Culebra Negro called out, and Cuchillo Colorado stopped and turned. He was only halfway to them, too far off for Fargo to reach in a quick bound.

Culebra Negro stood. Evidently he'd taken a fancy to Fargo's Henry and had it in his left hand. He came around the fire and over to Cuchillo Colorado and said something that caused Cuchillo Colorado to follow him off a short way where they hunkered and conversed.

"What do you suppose that's all about?" Charity whispered.

"No telling," Fargo said.

A third warrior unfurled, the one who had jumped Fargo on the hill. Fargo's Colt was wedged under his loincloth and he placed his hand on it as he walked to the horses, where, to Fargo's consternation, he patted the Ovaro's neck and raised a front leg and looked at the shoe and then ran his hand the length of the stallion's body.

"Someone likes your animal," Pratt whispered.

"Shhhh," Charity cautioned. "Here they come."

Cuchillo Colorado and Culebra Negro were walking toward them. The latter was smirking as he extended the Henry and said, "Your turn, white-eye."

The barrel was pointing at Fargo. "Me?" he said in surprise. He would have thought they'd take Pratt or Isaiah first.

It was Cuchillo Colorado who answered with, "You are not like these others. You are not weak. We kill you quick because you are brave."

"Some honor," Fargo said.

"What it is you whites say?" Cuchillo Colorado asked, and his eyes lit. "We save the best for last."

"You're a monster," Isaiah declared.

"Stand up, white-eye," Culebra Negro commanded, his finger around the Henry's trigger.

Fargo realized the hammer wasn't cocked. He glanced at the warrior over by the Ovaro and at the three still at the fire and decided there would be no better time. "Careful with that," he stalled. "I don't want you shooting me by mistake."

"Up," Culebra Negro barked.

Fargo rose to his knees. "You won't get away with this. The army will hunt you down no matter where you go."

"Let the blue coats hunt us," Cuchillo Colorado said, and laughed.

Culebra Negro was growing impatient. He took another step. "Up."

"Up it is," Fargo said. He rose slowly, awkwardly, to give the impression he was hampered by not having the use of his hands to keep his balance.

And then, when he was almost upright, he exploded into motion.

Sidestepping in case the Henry went off, Fargo grabbed the Henry and wrenched even as he drove the Arkansas toothpick into Culebra Negro's ribs. Culebra Negro stiffened and jerked and the toothpick slid out. With it came a spray of blood.

Cuchillo Colorado speared his fingers to his knife. He didn't quite have it clear of its sheath when Pratt sprang and tried to stab him in the throat. Leaping back, Cuchillo Colorado saved himself but was nicked deep enough to draw blood.

A bellow from an Apache at the fire brought all three to their feet.

Fargo pulled harder on the Henry. Culebra Negro was staggering, astonishment writ on his face. He tried to hold on but couldn't.

Fargo worked the lever and shot an onrushing warrior, jacked the lever again and shot a second. The third was almost on him and he had to skip back as he pumped the lever a third time. Thrusting the muzzle at the warrior's chest, he squeezed the trigger.

Pratt and Cuchillo Colorado were on the ground, grappling.

Fargo turned as the warrior who had been examining the Ovaro reached them. He brought up the Henry but the Apache was on him before he could fire. He was bowled over with the warrior on top. The Apache wrapped a hand on his throat while simultaneously trying to bury a blade in his belly. The Henry's stock deflected it and Fargo let go and grabbed the warrior's wrist. He heard Charity scream and slammed his knee into the warrior in an effort to knock him off.

"Leave her be!" Isaiah William shouted.

Fargo focused on the warrior and nothing else. He was using all his strength, but by gradual degrees the blade was being pressed closer and closer to his gut. He felt the prick of the tip just as he managed to roll out from under.

The warrior scrambled to his hands and knees, and attacked.

Fargo parried and steel rang on steel. He did some scrambling of his own to put space between them but the Apache came after him, stabbing, slashing. His arm stung with pain and his knuckle was opened.

"Nooooooo!" Charity cried.

Fargo didn't dare look. He blocked an overhand blow, pivoted, and raked the toothpick across the warrior's knife arm. Red drops flew. As quick as thought, the warrior flicked the knife to his other hand and came at Fargo again.

It was all Fargo could do to keep from being stabbed. He was forced to retreat.

The Apache gave a high bound and brought his blade curving down in a powerful slash. Slipping under the blow, Fargo lanced his toothpick up and in. It caught the warrior under the chin. The weight of the Apache's heavy body nearly drove Fargo to his knees as he drove the toothpick in as deep as it would go.

The warrior's eyes widened. Blood spurted. His arms sagged and he slumped and tried to speak but all that came out was more blood.

153

Fargo sprang away, yanking the toothpick out. The man thudded at his boots and he whirled to see how the others were faring.

Isaiah was on his back, his legs splayed, his eyes wide in death. He had been stabbed in the chest, in the heart.

On her knees next to him, clutching a knife smeared with scarlet, Charity was weeping. Her dress was splattered with red but none of it appeared to be hers.

Pratt was on his back, too. He'd been cut from his crotch to his sternum and some of his organs had oozed out. Incredibly, he was still alive. His eyes caught Fargo's and his mouth moved.

The Apaches were down, none moving. Fargo felt safe in moving to Pratt and squatting and bending his ear low to hear.

"Cut . . . him . . . good . . ." Pratt said, barely loud enough to hear. The next moment he died.

Only then did Fargo realize that Cuchillo Colorado wasn't among the fallen warriors. Jumping up, he reclaimed the Henry and came back to where Pratt lay.

Splashes of blood led off across the basin, growing larger as they went.

Fargo couldn't understand why Cuchillo Colorado hadn't used a horse instead of escaping on foot. Then it hit him. The wound must be fatal, or close to it, and Cuchillo Colorado was going off to die. Apaches, when mortally stricken, often did like dying wolves would do and found a private spot to breathe their last.

Fargo needed to be sure. "Stay here," he said to Charity. He'd taken only a few strides when she called his name.

"Where are you going? You can't leave me here alone."

"Cuchillo Colorado," Fargo said, thinking that would be enough.

"What about him?"

Fargo pointed at the trail of blood. "He's still alive."

"My brother isn't," Charity said, and fresh tears flowed. "Did you see what he did?"

Chafing at the delay, Fargo shook his head.

"An Apache was coming at me and Isaiah threw himself in front of him. He took a knife meant for me." Charity said

154

it as if she could hardly believe it. "He gave his life to save mine."

Fargo didn't know what to say. Even cowards sometimes showed a spark of courage.

"I never would have thought he had it in him. He hated violence. He was such a sweet person. You should have seen him when—"

"Charity," Fargo cut her off.

She looked at him in confusion.

"I don't have time for this. Cuchillo Colorado, remember?"

"Oh." Charity blinked, and dabbed at her tears. "Yes. By all means. Go after him. But do me a favor."

Fargo waited.

"Don't let him kill you."

46

The sun was boiling the land alive. Thanks to the heat, the drops had dried within moments of falling. Some were as big around as silver dollars.

Fargo followed them for over a mile. Most men would have long since collapsed. Most whites, anyway. Apaches were hardier, and Cuchillo Colorado was one of the hardiest.

The hills gave way to a maze of boulders and washes.

Fargo had the impression Cuchillo Colorado was searching for something. Maybe a hole to crawl into, or some other spot where his body would never be found.

He was deep in the maze when he came to a flat area about an acre wide. The drops led toward the other side. He was halfway across when, to his consternation, the drops ended.

He stopped and studied the ground ahead and to the right and the left. Nothing. It couldn't be, he told himself. It was almost as if Cuchillo Colorado had bled himself dry. But in that case, he'd be lying there lifeless.

Belatedly, another possibility dawned, and sent a ripple of ice down Fargo's spine.

It could be that Cuchillo Colorado had staunched the flow of blood. Only why wait until now and not do it sooner? The only reason Fargo could think of was that Cuchillo Colorado *wanted* to leave a trail. That the wily Apache expected to be followed and had made it easy until this point.

Until Fargo was out in the open, exposed, as good a target as a man could ask for.

And Cuchillo Colorado had his Colt.

Fargo started to turn even as a gun boomed. His hat went sailing and he felt as he were punched in the head. His legs gave and he fell. He lay still, feigning death while he tried to collect his wits. His left hand was near enough to his head that he could touch it without moving his arm. He was fortunate in that the slug had glanced off. His head hurt like hell and he'd have another scar but he'd live.

Giving silent thanks that Apaches seldom used six-shooters, he heaved up and ran back the way he came. The Colt boomed a second time, but the shot missed. There was time for a third but Cuchillo Colorado didn't try.

Reaching a boulder, Fargo ducked behind it. He was caked with sweat and blood was trickling onto his ear.

Swatting at a fly, he waited to catch his breath.

"You hear me, white-eye?"

The bellow came from a tangle of boulders that could conceal a grizzly.

"I hear you," Fargo replied, surprised that Cuchillo Colorado would give his position away.

"I almost kill you."

"You almost did," Fargo admitted.

"That other one, the one who hurt Corn Flower, he is dead, yes?"

"Yes."

"Good."

Fargo studied the tangle, figuring how best to reach it without taking lead.

"White-eye?" Cuchillo Colorado called.

"I'm still here," Fargo hollered.

"I die soon. You go so I die alone."

"I have to be sure."

"You think maybe I lie? You think maybe I live to kill more whites?"

"There's that," Fargo said, and swore he heard a chuckle.

Silence fell.

Ducking as low as he could go, Fargo moved around the boulder, tensed, and flew to another. The next was too far away to risk running, so he flattened and crawled. He was

157

almost to it when the Colt spanged and lead sent chips flying.

The hot breeze brought another chuckle.

It was unusual, an Apache doing that.

Fargo didn't think anything more of it and continued to work into the tangle. The boulders were in a jumble with some on top of others, and often he had to squeeze through gaps that caused him to lose whangs off his buckskins and more than a little skin.

Twice the Colt cracked, and each time the slug came within a hair of ending his life. And after each shot he heard another of those damnable chuckles.

By Fargo's reckoning Cuchillo Colorado now had only one shot left. Fargo figured he'd wait until he couldn't miss.

A gully offered temporary safety. It also wound toward the spot the shots came from.

As silently as a cougar, Fargo stalked his quarry. He came to the shadow of a giant slab and eased high enough to peer over.

Cuchillo Colorado wasn't five feet away, his back propped against the slab, a grin on his face and the Colt in his lap.

Fargo brought up the Henry but caught himself.

Cuchillo Colorado hadn't moved. His eyes were glazed, and his grin was no such thing. It was a death grimace, an involuntary contortion at the point of dying.

Rising, Fargo went over. He felt for a pulse that wasn't there. Prying the Colt from Cuchillo Colorado's stiffening fingers, he hefted it and thought about the near misses, and wondered. He stared at the body and said, "Damn you."

It was a simple matter to drag him to the shallow wash but not so simple to find enough small rocks and loose dirt to cover him with.

By the time he was done, Fargo was caked with dust and exhausted to his marrow.

He bent his steps to the basin.

Charity was still beside her brother, awash in despair. She didn't rise to meet him. "Is he . . . ?"

"He is," Fargo said.

"Will you help me take my brother home to bury him?"

Fargo nodded.

"I wouldn't mind if you stuck around a while. I can use the company. What do you say?"

For once in his life Fargo didn't grin or wink or make a remark about her luscious body. All he did was wearily wipe the sweat from his eyes and say, "Makes two of us."

LOOKING FORWARD!
The following is the opening section of the next novel in the exciting Trailsman series from Signet:

TRAILSMAN #388
BORDERLAND BLOODBATH

Rio Grande borderland, 1860—where Skye Fargo witnesses an international land grab and ends up stalked by the most fearsome assassin on the frontier.

The Ovaro gave his low trouble whicker, jolting Skye Fargo out of an uneasy sleep.

In one fluid, continuous movement only a heartbeat after his eyes snapped open, Fargo rolled out of his blanket, rose to a low crouch, shucked his walnut-grip Colt from his holster and thumb-cocked it.

At first, as the last cobwebs of sleep cleared from his mind, all seemed calm enough. Cicadas gave off their metronomic, singsong rhythm; the nearby Rio Grande purled gently only ten yards away; a fat full moon had turned from the buttery color of early evening to the pale white that preceded dawn.

Then Fargo heard it: a man's authoritative voice snapping out an indistinct command from about fifty yards upriver.

The Ovaro snorted, not liking this mysterious human intrusion.

"Steady on, old campaigner," Fargo said in a low voice, placing a hand on the stallion's neck to calm him. "Whoever they are, they don't know we're here."

It was 1860, the middle of the blistering dog days in the American Southwest, and the man some called the Trailsman had just finished a three-month stint riding security for a merchant caravan between Santa Fe and Guadalajara, Mexico. He had collected his final pay earlier in El Paso and pitched camp for the night in this juniper thicket on the American side of the sleepy, muddy, meandering river Mexicans called Rio Bravo del Norte, Americans Rio Grande.

Another voice rang out upriver and again Fargo couldn't make out the words. But for some inexplicable reason an ominous sense of foreboding prickled his scalp.

"You picked the wrong campsite, Fargo," he muttered.

It wasn't just these voices now. Earlier, when Fargo was cleaning and oiling his brass-framed Henry rifle, a lone rider had moved in close, forcing Fargo to kick dirt over his small fire.

Still, such a level of activity was hardly surprising along the U.S.-Mexico border. *Contrabandistas*, slave-trading Comancheros, whiskey peddlers, and gunrunners operated with impunity in this area, and they naturally preferred the cloak of darkness. Whoever they were, Fargo figured it was none of his mix.

Again the commanding voice and this time Fargo thought he had heard the English words "shore it up."

He moved cautiously forward out of the thicket, unpleasantly aware once again of a vaguely foreboding premonition of danger. Despite the warm night his skin goose-bumped, stiffening the hair on his forearms.

Something's wrong, Fargo, insisted an urgent inner voice. *Something's dead wrong. Don't you notice what it is?*

Fargo emerged silently from the thicket and saw the river reflecting glimmering points of color in the moonlight despite being at its muddiest by late summer. He glanced upriver and spotted torches burning. But he couldn't see much because the black velvet folds of darkness seemed to absorb the illumination before it reached his eyes.

More words reached him now, muffled by the distance and the constant chuckling of the river: ". . . use plenty . . . not too deep . . . more past the bend . . ."

Occasionally he spotted ghostly figures moving in and out of the light. He listened carefully to a steady chunking sound and recognized it as several shovels digging. Men burying contraband, maybe, but why so close to the water?

What's wrong, Fargo? that insistent inner voice demanded again from some layer of awareness located in survival reflex, not conscious thought. *Figure it out fast, man, before it's too late!*

Fargo tucked at the knees beside the river growth and moved slowly closer to the men. Again he reminded himself it was none of his picnic, that he might be edging closer to something immensely dangerous, but intense curiosity had him in its grip.

Fargo realized the shoveling had stopped and suddenly the torches were snuffed. Moments later he heard the rataplan of iron-shod hooves as the men escaped to the north.

But escaping from who?

Not who, Fargo, urged that body voice deeper than thought. *Escaping from* what? *Snap into it, Trailsman! Don't you understand what's wrong?*

Fargo halted as his mind, honed by years of deadly scrapes and narrow escapes, frantically assembled the baffling clues. The shovels, the sudden escape, the half-formed words he might or might not have heard correctly: "Shore it up . . . use plenty . . . not too deep . . . more past the bend . . ."

And this sudden, throbbing silence . . .

Silence!

"God*damn*," Fargo abruptly whispered as the important clue he had missed now slammed into him like a fist, something taught to him years ago by an old mountain man: "Watch out, boy, when the insects fall silent."

Fargo realized what was coming and turned on his heel,

bolting back toward the juniper thicket as his stomach turned into a ball of ice. Even as he was about to dive into the thicket the peaceful night was split by blinding light and a cracking boom like the promised doom clap of final reckoning.

The earth split open and heaved flames and dirt in a towering column into the sky. Fargo heard the terrified neighing of the Ovaro and felt a searing ripple of heat as the fire surge washed over him before lifting him into the night and flinging him like a child's toy.

You were too late, Fargo, was his last thought before his world closed down to pain and darkness and oblivion. *You were just a few seconds too late!*

THE LAST OUTLAWS
The Lives and Legends of Butch Cassidy and the Sundance Kid

by Thom Hatch

Butch Cassidy and the Sundance Kid are two of the most celebrated figures of American lore. As leaders of the Wild Bunch, also known as the Hole-in-the-Wall Gang, they planned and executed the most daring bank and train robberies of the day, with an uprecedented professionalism.

The Last Outlaws brilliantly brings to life these thrilling, larger-than-life personalities like never before, placing the legend of Butch and Sundance in the context of a changing—and shrinking—American West, as the rise of 20th century technology brought an end to a remarkable era. Drawing on a wealth of fresh research, Thom Hatch pushes aside the myth and offers up a compelling, fresh look at these icons of the Wild West.

Available wherever books are sold or at penguin.com

S0464

National bestselling author

RALPH COMPTON

"A writer in the tradition of Louis L'Amour and Zane Grey!" —*Huntsville Times*

Available wherever books are sold or at
penguin.com

S543